T0065260

INDIAN
WARFARE

INDIAN WARFARE

Heart of a warrior

BLACK MALE

INDIAN WARFARE
HEART OF A WARRIOR

iUniverse books may be ordered through booksellers or by contacting:

iUniverse
1663 Liberty Drive
Bloomington, IN 47403
www.iuniverse.com
844-349-9409

ISBN: 978-1-6632-2584-9 (sc)
ISBN: 978-1-6632-2585-6 (e)

Print information available on the last page.

iUniverse rev. date: 08/17/2021

CONTENTS

Characters at the end.

INDIAN WARFARE HISTORY
(How the Indians got their powers)

In the 15th century, the Europeans came to America thinking they were in India. When they invaded Arkansas, they saw red-skinned people with paint on their faces and feathers in their hair. The Europeans thought they were weird. The so-called Indians thought the same. They were looking for new land to take over. They and the Indians became friends at first. The Europeans propositioned the Indians with money and weapons for their land, but the Indians refused to sale it.

The Europeans was enraged, and thought if they wouldn't sale their land, then they would take it. So, without warning, the Europeans attacked and went to war with the Indians for their land.

There were two dominant Indian tribes in Arkansas. The Kwawpaw and the Ahshitaw. The Kwawpaw tribe were peaceful and didn't fight unless they were threatened. The Ahshitaw tribe were more aggressive. They would fight if they were threatened or not. The Europeans had more weapons than the Indian people had, and were winning the war. Between the Kwawpaw and Ahshitaw territories, a diamond shaped bright red gem was planted in the ground. If that gem were removed, humanity would be cursed with animal instincts, which means if someone were angered, they would turn into the animal they liked. The Kwawpaw and Ahshitaw tribes came together and agreed to remove the gem and go to battle with the Europeans and run them from their land. The Indian chiefs removed the gem and a lot of bright red smoke came from the ground, covered the earth, and gave every human being in the world a power to change into an animal when they are angered.

The Europeans changed into animals, but they were weaker. The Kwawpaw and Ahshitaw tribes were stronger and eventually ran the Europeans away from their land. The Ahshitaw tribe became greedy and tried to take over the Kwawpaw tribe land.

The Kwawpaw Indians were well organized and smarter than the Ahshitaw tribe was. The chief of the Ahshitaw tribe decided to sale his soul to Nukpana, (The Devil) to defeat the Chief of the Kwawpaw tribe. If the chief win, he would own the Kwawpaw territory. If the Ahshitaw chief loses, he will go to hell. The chiefs of the Kwawpaw and Ahshitaw had a battle.

The chief of the Ahshitaw tribe lost. When his soul left his body, instead of him going to hell, he tried to possess the Kwawpaw chief's body. The Kwawpaw chief had a round medallion around his neck. When the Ahshitaw chief tried to enter the Kwawpaw chief's body, his soul entered into the medallion. If that medallion is taken off, then humanity will be cursed with animal instincts again. Before a Kwawpaw chief dies, he has to pray and pass the medallion down to the new generation.

That was the first war. The second one was civil. Now a third war is about to begin. This time it is going to be more serious.

ACKNOWLEDGEMENTS

I got to thank God for the blessings and the gift for me to be a writer. I've influenced a lot of people, even the ones across seas. I got people from Africa, California, Chicago, France, Germany, Louisiana, Italy, Miami, New York, Texas, and the Philippines that's telling me that there my fans. Thanks! Rest in love to my mother and father, Ms. Eva Mae Holly & Joe D. Young. And all my brothers and sisters that has passed on. The latest was Nathaniel Holly.

Shout out to Rhonda for my book cover and to Junrey Buena for helping me to draw out the characters.

To everybody who bought all five of my albums, and my books. I really appreciate that. Y'all are genuine fans.

Since you supported me, I got some more music coming out later called "Unheard Hits!" in 2021. To all upcoming Rappers, R&B Singers, book writers or whatever you want to be, don't let nobody tell you what you can and can't do. Stay away from people who will show you, **Fake Luv (Fake Friends).** They'll turn on you in a second. "Oh Yeah!" I got to give a big shout out to Coast to Coast F.M. radio station in Miami Florida for playing my music in rotation.

To all you entrepreneurs out there, invest your money into yourself if you want to be successful at something, and don't depend on nobody to help you to do anything.

Indian Warfare is going to be the next thing in the future.

To everybody who tried to hate and sabotage me, I told you I can't be stopped. I'm a B.O.S.S. I won the battle and the war.

Chapter 1

BATTLE CRY

There are two new leaders of each tribe. Chief White Eagle is the leader of the Kwawpaw tribe. Chief Serpent is the leader of the Ahshitaw tribe. Chief Serpent pretends that he wants to battle Chief White Eagle for his land, but he really wants the medallion around his neck. Chief White Eagle has a white, and yellow Indian hat made of feathers on his head.

The white represents peace within the Kwawpaw tribe. The yellow represents the power of the sun. He wears a black jacket, black pants, yellow shoes on, and a knife tied to his belt.

Chief Serpent has the same Indian hat made of feathers on his head. The feathers on his hat are green and black.

The green represents poisonous snakes. The black represents death to his enemies. He has maroon paint across his face, and two lines down on both sides of his jaw. Chief Serpent is known to be treacherous and would attack anybody at any time. He has a green tank top made of snake scales on with two knives on both sides of his boots. They're meeting up on a mountain top. They have their sons with them as witnesses. Chief White Eagle son name is Gray Wolf. He has a white feather on the back of his head. He has hair that comes to his shoulders. Black war paint across his eyes. A gray jacket with black strings hanging down from his arms of his jacket. He has gray pants on with the same strings hanging down from his leg, and gray shoes.

Chief Serpent son name is Redd Lion. He has a black Mohawk with the top of his hair dyed red. He has black circle like paint around his eyes with two lines on each side of his jaw. This is war paint signaling that he has already killed somebody. He talks with a deep voice. You have no choice but to take him seriously when he's speaking.

He's wearing a red tank top, red pants with black strings on the side, with red shoes on. He's a little taller, vicious, and muscular than Gray Wolf. He and Gray Wolf use to play together as kids until they turned eighteen. Their fathers made them stop playing together because they had to learn the traditions of their tribe, and they might become enemies one day.

Chief White Eagle and Gray Wolf was coming from the west. Chief Serpent and Redd Lion was coming from the East.

They met on a mountaintop between the Kwawpaw and Ahshitaw territories. Chief White Eagle took his feathered hat off and gave it to Gray Wolf. He has solid long white hair coming past his shoulder. Chief Serpent took his feathered hat off and gave it to Redd Lion. He has a Gray-haired Mohawk. He and Chief White Eagle met up face to face. Chief White Eagle asked what do you want Serpent? Chief Serpent said one more battle for your Kwawpaw territory. Chief White Eagle said I'm not stupid, you don't want my territory. You want this medallion off my neck. Chief Serpent said my ancestor spirit is in that medallion, and he need to be freed.

Chief White Eagle said your ancestor spirit has turned into a demon. If this medallion is taken off my neck, humanity will be cursed with animal instincts again. Once you sell your soul to Nukpana (The Devil), bad things always happen. Chief Serpent said no it won't, It's a myth. We can pray and transfer the medallion from your neck to mine. Chief White Eagle talked with anger. He replied, yes it will! It happened before and it will happen again.

I will battle you one more time. This time if I win, you will never return to challenge me for my land or medallion again. Chief Serpent said o.k. it's a deal.

Chief White Eagle and Chief Serpent faced each other. Since they were chiefs, they had powers; Chief White Eagle had lightning that came from his hands. Chief Serpent had light green strings that came from his hands and will make you weak if you're hit. As they faced and stirred at each other, Chief Serpent charged at Chief White Eagle throwing punches and kicks.

Chief White Eagle blocked his punches and kicks. He counter attacked and struck him in the face and chest. They were both in their late 50's, but they fought as if they were in their early 20's. Chief Serpent kept throwing punches and kicks, but was not landing in punches. Chief White Eagle threw lightning from his hands and struck Chief Serpent in the chest and knocked him to the ground. As Chief Serpent laid on the ground, Chief White Eagle talked to him. He said I beat you in this round. If I beat you again, I win.

Chief Serpent got up as they fought again. Chief White Eagle blocked his punches, but he left one of his guards down as Chief Serpent threw green strings from his hands hitting Chief White Eagle in the chest as he kneeled down on one knee.

Chief Serpent ran towards Chief White Eagle as he threw lightning from his hands, striking Chief Serpent in the legs and chest. Chief Serpent was too weak to fight again. He was on his knees as Chief White Eagle walked up to him.

He ignited electricity from both of his hands forming into lightning. He could have killed Chief Serpent easily.

Chief Serpent said o.k. White Eagle, you win. Chief White Eagle said now leave. I don't want you and your members to return. Gray Wolf was excited about his father winning. He yelled out to his father. Yeah! I knew you could beat him! Redd Lion said to Gray Wolf, shut up! It's not over yet!

Chief White Eagle turned around and looked at Gray Wolf. When he did, Chief Serpent pulled a knife from his boot and stabbed Chief White Eagle in the chest. Chief White Eagle fell on one knee, pulled his knife from his belt, jumped up and stabbed Chief Serpent in his chest. Gray Wolf hollered "No!" as he ran towards his father and Chief Serpent.

Redd Lion jumped in, and ran towards Gray Wolf. When Gray Wolf got close to Chief White Eagle and Chief Serpent, Redd Lion did a jump kick, striking Gray Wolf in the chest and knocked him to the ground. Redd Lion walked up to Chief White Eagle and Chief Serpent, pulling them apart. He laid Chief Serpent down and pulled the knife out of his chest.

He looked back at Chief White Eagle and saw the medallion. He ran up and snatched it off of his neck. When he did, this bright red light came from it. Then all of a sudden, the medallion busted and red smoke came from it and covered the whole planet, giving every human being animal instinct.

When someone is angered, they will turn into an animal. Redd Lion couldn't believe what had happened. When all the smoke was clearing, he picked Chief Serpent up and carried him off.

Gray Wolf and Chief White Eagle were laying on the ground. Gray Wolf got up and saw all this bright red smoke clearing up.

He looked over at Chief White Eagle and saw the knife stuck in his chest, and he wasn't moving. Gray Wolf ran over, pulled the knife out, and picked him up to carry him to the Kwawpaw reservation. As Gray Wolf was carrying Chief White Eagle, he noticed that he had gotten stronger. His sense of hearing, seeing, smelling, tasting, and he was mentally and physically stronger as if an extra energy was within him. He started crying because he knew his father was going to die.

As Gray Wolf was walking, Chief White Eagle moaned. He could barely talk, he said to Gray Wolf, you have to get that medallion back. If it's not back in two days, mankind will be cursed with animal instincts forever.

Gray Wolf said I will get it back. I promise.

Chief White Eagle closed his eyes and died in Gray Wolf's arms. His spirit left his body as an outline of a bright glow was around his soul. Gray Wolf couldn't believe that he's looking at his father's spirit floating in the air above his head. Chief White Eagle said be careful Gray Wolf. You are a warrior now. I trust that you will do what's right. Now I'm giving you my powers to throw lightning from your hands to stop your enemies from hurting you.

Gray Wolf said thank you, and I will.

Lightning came from Chief White Eagle's soul to Gray Wolfs as his spirit went to heaven. Gray Wolf looked at his father's body in his arms on his way to the Kwawpaw territory. When he finally made it, the first person he saw was his girlfriend, Aiyana. She has two pony tails in the front, hanging down from her head to her breast.

She has on a gray dress, and gray shoes on. When she saw Gray Wolf carrying his father's body, she immediately started crying. She ran to Gray Wolf, and asked, what happened? Gray Wolf said he and Chief Serpent killed each other in battle, and it's my fault. Aiyana asked how is it your fault? Gray Wolf said I distracted him when he beat Chief Serpent. When he turned and looked at me, Chief Serpent pulled a knife and stabbed him in the chest.

But my dad stabbed him back in his chest, and they both fell. Aiyana said oh my God! Gray Wolf asked Aiyana, have you seen Uncle Hawk? She said yes, he's talking to his son, Wolvie by his tipi.

Gray Wolf and Aiyana walked to find his Uncle Hawk. They walked and found him by a tipi. Hawk who is dressed in all brown clothing with a bow in one hand, with arrows on his back. He's an expert with bow and arrows. He has gray hair down to his shoulders. He's blind in his left eye because Chief Serpent spit venom in his eye in the last battle. Hawk is the most feared warrior in the Kwawpaw tribe. Even the Ahshitaw fighters gave him respect because he killed a quite a few of their members. If he defeats you, he would kill you with no hesitation. He can form tornado winds from the ground. When dirt gets in your eye, he would give you a brutal attack. He has two brown feathers in the back of his head.

One feather means that he's a Kwawpaw warrior. The other one means he's next in line to be the chief of the Kwawpaw tribe. As Gray Wolf and Aiyana got closer, Gray Wolf called out to his Uncle, yelling, Uncle Hawk! Uncle Hawk!

Hawk turned around and saw Gray Wolf carrying Chief White Eagle's body. He dropped his bow and ran to Gray Wolf.

Hawk asked, what happened? Gray Wolf said he and Chief Serpent killed each other in battle. Hawk couldn't believe his brother was dead. He looked Gray Wolf in the eye. He said let's get everybody together and bury him.

Gray Wolf said o.k.

Hawk, Gray Wolf, and Aiyana got everybody from the Kwawpaw tribe together and buried Chief White Eagle. When somebody die or is killed in the Kwawpaw tribe, they are buried immediately. After the burial, Hawk escorted Gray Wolf and Aiyana to their tipi.

Hawk said to Gray Wolf, get you some rest, and we will decide what we're going to do tomorrow. Gray Wolf said o.k. I will.

Aiyana said thanks Hawk, as he went to his tipi. Gray Wolf and Aiyana laid down. They went to sleep almost at the same time.

Chapter 2

GRAY WOLF

The next day, Gray Wolf was sleeping, having a dream about the murder of his father and how Chief Serpent stabbed him to death. When he saw the knife enter into his father's chest and how Redd Lion snatched off the medallion.

Gray Wolf jumped out of his sleep. Aiyana walked in the tipi as Gray Wolf was waking up. She was bringing him water and eggs for him to eat. She put the food in front of him. Aiyana asked are you O.K.? Gray Wolf said no, not really. I got to figure out how to get that medallion back. Aiyana said don't worry about it, you'll get it back.

Gray Wolf said you don't understand, I got to get it back in two days. She asked, why?

He said yesterday, did you see all that red smoke that came over the mountains? Aiyana said yeah, the smoke covered everything. Gray Wolf said that smoke came from my father's medallion. We supposed to have powers to turn into animals when we are angered now. It's weird because my father told me a couple of years ago that he had a dream about he and Chief Serpent killing each other in battle and it happened. Now me and Redd Lion are going to be enemies. My father gave him his nickname when we use to play together as kids.

Aiyana looked at Gray Wolf as if he was crazy. She asked, are you being serious? Gray Wolf said yeah, and it's because of that medallion. Do you feel stronger? She said yeah, I feel like there's an extra energy in me. He said that's because it is. Your animal form is within you, and you always like foxes. As Gray Wolf and Aiyana were talking, they heard a voice outside of their tipi calling Gray Wolf's name. He and Aiyana walked outside and it was his Uncle Hawk. He was walking up to their tipi.

Gray Wolf asked, what's going on Hawk? His Uncle Hawk said I just came from over by the Ahshitaw territory. People are telling me that Redd Lion is recruiting fighters and they're not all Indian. They're fighters from different nationalities. Gray Wolf said really?! Hawk said yes really. I think he's trying to take over the Kwawpaw territory. I don't know how many fighters he has, but he has to be stopped. Gray Wolf said yeah, you're right, so what's the first move I have to do? Hawk said you're going to have to recruit your own fighters. They don't have to be all Indian. Just recruit the brave, fast and strong ones.

Gray Wolf asked what about you, do you want to come with me? Hawk said I'm too old, plus we're outnumbered. I have to stay here and protect the Kwawpaw territory. Aiyana asked what about your son, Wolvie?

Hawk said he's not ready. He's still in training. He's short tempered and he don't listen sometimes. He's starting to act like a real Wolverine. Gray Wolf asked why do we turn into animals? Hawk said when earth is cursed with animal instincts, you will turn into the animal that you always liked.

As Hawk, Gray Wolf, and Aiyana were talking, a strange smell of cologne and sweat was in the air.

Gray Wolf asked do you smell that. Aiyana said yeah, it smells like cologne. Hawk replied, and sweat.

As Gray Wolf, Aiyana, and Hawk was talking, they heard a voice behind them saying hello, and how are you doing? Gray

Wolf, Aiyana, and Hawk turned around and it was a bald head white male with blue eyes and a scar on his left jaw in a maroon and white jump suit walking towards them. Gray Wolf stepped forward and asked, who are you? The man in the maroon jump suit said my name is Tommy. I just became a member of the Ahshitaw tribe. Gray Wolf yelled, the Ahshitaw tribe! You're associated with Redd Lion? Tommy said yes, he recruited me.

Gray Wolf got wide eyed. He asked Tommy, where is he? He has something that belongs to me.

Tommy started laughing. He replied he's around. He's very close. Gray Wolf said you either tell me where he's at or I'm going to force you to tell me.

Tommy said well that's what you're going to have to do. Gray Wolf and Tommy faced each other, getting ready to fight. They glared at one another for about three seconds. They rushed each other. They punched and kicked each other back and forward for ten seconds until they both went into their animal rage.

Gray Wolf let out a roar and turned into an Alaskan Gray Wolf. He looked somewhat like a werewolf, but more Alaskan. When he transformed, he howled like wolves do.

He was two toned-gray. He was dark gray on top of his head, and light gray below his eyes. He was muscular and had claws, paws, and a bushy light gray tail. Tommy let out a roar and turned into a Warthog. He had big teeth that came up out of his mouth. He was muscular with hands like a human and feet like a hog. Aiyana put her hands to her mouth not believing what she's seeing. Gray Wolf and Tommy are facing each other in their animal form. Gray Wolf started growling and showing his teeth. Tommy said get ready to lose this battle. When humans turn into their animal form, they can talk in their regular voice. He squealed like a hog as they rushed each other. They were punching and kicking each other for several minutes.

Gray Wolf turned back human. Tommy was still in his animal form. He charged, but Gray Wolf threw lightning from his hands striking Tommy in the chest as he hit the ground. When he did, he turned back human. Gray Wolf couldn't believe what had happened because this the first time he turned into his animal form and throwing lightning from his hands. Tommy got up from the ground. Gray Wolf said now tell me where Redd Lion is.

Tommy said he's around. He's getting ready to take over this land. Tommy got up off the ground and ran down the hill. Gray

Wolf was getting ready to chase after him until Hawk called him. He yelled, Gray Wolf! Gray Wolf!

Gray Wolf said he know where Redd Lion is. Hawk said he might be setting you up. He might have more fighters down the hill. Gray Wolf thought about it for a minute. He came back towards Hawk and Aiyana.

Aiyana said you have an animal in you. Hawk said all of us do. The earth is cursed with animal instincts.

Gray Wolf asked so what do we do now. Hawk said you're going to have to recruit your own fighters. There's no telling how many fighters Redd Lion has. Gray Wolf asked do you know any fighters. Hawk said Yeah, I know one. He lives down the hill where that guy ran towards. His name is Tauro. He's a farmer from Mexico. He's very serious. I don't think he has a sense of humor at all. You might have to challenge him to a duel.

Gray Wolf asked, why? Hawk said that's how we recruit fighters. If you win, he joins you. If you lose, you leave it's that simple. Gray Wolf said well I got to do what I got to do. Aiyana said you mean you're leaving now.

Gray Wolf said Yeah, I have to. I got two days to get that medallion back and stop Redd Lion from taking our land.

Aiyana hugged and kissed Gray Wolf because she didn't know if she was going to see him again. Hawk shook Gray Wolf's hand and said good luck. Gray Wolf said thanks because I'm going to need it. He took off walking down the hill to recruit the fighter named Tauro.

Chapter 3

TAURO

As he was walking down the hill, Hawk called him. He hollered out, Gray Wolf! As he turned around to see what he wanted. He asked Hawk, what's wrong? Hawk said If you're out and it turns dark, put your index finger to your temper and your night vision will come one. You can see at night, and see foot prints in the dirt in case you're tracking somebody. Gray Wolf said thanks Uncle Hawk.

After Hawk told him that, he went back to his tipi as Gray Wolf went down the hill to meet the fighter named Tauro. Gray Wolf got to the end of the hill. He looked to his right and seen a guy a little shorter than him wearing a sombrero hat chopping wood. Gray Wolf walked up behind him. The guy that was chopping wood, turned around and got startled. He had diamond shaped designs in front of his sombrero with the colors of red, white, and green. The colors of the Mexican flag. He had on a long sleeve button up red shirt on with a brown vest, brown pants, and red shoes on.

He had a thick mustache and a goatee. He had a look on his face like he means business. The man wearing the Sombrero asked, who are you? Gray Wolf spoke and introduced himself. He said I'm the son of Chief White Eagle of the Kwawpaw tribe.

The man wearing the Sombrero said I heard of Chief White Eagle and the Kwawpaw tribe. He had a brother named Hawk.

Gray Wolf said yes Hawk is my uncle. He sent me down here to talk to someone named Tauro.

The farmer looked at Gray Wolf with piercing eyes. He said that's me. What do you want? You know you're the second person that came through here trespassing on my property. Gray Wolf said this is Kwawpaw territory. All of this land belongs to us. You say I'm the second person that came through here, who was the first person?

Tauro said some bald head guy in a maroon and white jump suit. Gray Wolf said that sounds like the guy I had the altercation with. Did he try to recruit you? Tauro said no, I just told him to stay off my land.

Gray Wolf said o.k. I heard you are a good fighter. I need you to join me to get my father's medallion back.

Tauro asked, are you kidding me? You want me to help you get some necklace back?

Gray Wolf said you don't understand, this is no regular necklace. Earth is cursed with animal instincts now. When you get angry, you're going to turn into an animal.

Tauro said amigo, you been watching too many sci-fi movies. What's in it for me?

Gray Wolf said I tell you what, I'll challenge you to a duel. If I win, you join me. If you win, I'll leave and never return. Tauro asked, are you sure, you want to challenge me? Gray Wolf said yeah, I'm sure. I need all the fighters I can get.

Tauro threw the axe down and said let's do it. He and Gray Wolf faced each other, getting ready to fight.

Tauro charged at Gray Wolf at full speed throwing punches and kicks. Gray Wolf was blocking his punches and kicks, but then they started landing and Gray Wolf was getting hit. Gray Wolf blocked and threw counter punches and hitting him back.

Tauro threw knives at Gray Wolf as he ducked and threw lightning from both hands striking Tauro's feet and knocking him to the ground. Tauro got up and went into his animal rage. He put his hands to the side and let out a roar and turned into a bull.

Gray Wolf let out his roar and turning into his Alaskan Gray Wolf form. Tauro, who was muscular with two big black horns in front of his head. He started rubbing his right foot back and forth like a bull getting ready to charge. He started talking to Gray Wolf. He said you're in trouble amigo, you're going to lose.

Gray Wolf said oh yeah, then bring it. Tauro charged, but Gray Wolf got out the way. When Tauro ran passed him, Gray Wolf ran to him, throwing combo punches and kicks. Somehow Gray Wolf got the best of him. They both turned back human at the same time. Tauro couldn't believe he turned into a bull. He was trying to figure out what happened. Gray Wolf threw lightning from his hands, striking him in the chest and knocking him to the ground. Gray Wolf waited for a couple of seconds to see if he was going to get back up. The lightning weakened him. Gray Wolf walked up on Tauro and started talking.

He asked, now do you believe me. Tauro said yeah, I turned into a bull amigo.

Gray Wolf said yeah, that's the animal that you liked. Gray Wolf reached out with his hand to help Tauro get up.

He said to Gray Wolf, well a deal is a deal, I guess I got to join you. Gray Wolf said let me ask you something, do you know any more fighters? Tauro said yeah, I know one. I know a guy named Brazen, but he lives in the icy mountains. It's real cold up their amigo.

Gray Wolf said well we got to see if he'll join us. I got to hurry up and get that medallion back.

Tauro said amigo, we can ride in my van. Gray Wolf said o.k. let's go.

Gray Wolf and Tauro got in the van and rode to the icy mountains to meet the fighter called Brazen.

Chapter 4

BRAZEN

Gray Wolf and Tauro left the Kwawpaw territory to ride up north to the icy mountains. As soon as they arrived, they noticed how hard it was snowing. Tauro parked the van in the mushy snow because he didn't want to run into the slippery ice. He and Gray Wolf got out the van to search for the man named Brazen.

Tauro asked how are we supposed to find somebody in all of this snow. Gray Wolf said he can't be too far.

He thought about what his Uncle Hawk said about his night vision. He wondered if it would work in the snow. He put his index finger to his temper as his eyes started glowing with yellow light. He looked all around until he looked east. He saw smoke coming from a chimney. He took his finger off of his temper. He said to

Tauro: Come this way, there's a chimney over on the east. Tauro asked how do you know.

Gray Wolf said put your index finger to your temper and look east. Tauro put his finger to his temper as his eyes glowed bright yellow. He looked east as he saw the smoke coming from the chimney. Tauro said your right amigo, let's go this way.

Gray Wolf and Tauro walked east to the house with the smoke coming out the chimney. They walked until they saw the house. They were walking under a tree, but they didn't see the snow in it. The branch started cracking. They both looked up as the branch broke and the snow fell. They jumped out the way as the snow hit the ground.

Gray Wolf said that was a close call. Tauro replied yeah, I know. As they were still on the ground, they heard a voice behind them, asking: Can I help you?

Gray Wolf and Tauro got up from the ground. The guy they were talking to was a tall white male that stood over 6-foot-tall with a round Al Capone fedora hat on with a black stripe across it. He has on black shades with a white sweater, white pants, and white boots. Gray Wolf said yes, we're looking for someone named Brazen.

Tauro whispered to Gray Wolf. He said I think it's him. The man dressed in white looked at Tauro and said I know you don't I. Then he looked at Gray Wolf and asked, are you the police. Gray Wolf said no. He asked are you with the F.B.I, D.E.A, C.I.A or any other police agency. Gray Wolf said no, I'm looking for him to ask him something.

The man in white said o.k. Then I'm Brazen. What do you want? Gray Wolf said I'm looking for a fighter to come with me to help me get my father's medallion back. Brazen started laughing. Gray Wolf said you don't understand, the guy that has it, have some fighters with him, and I'm pretty sure they'll all come at me trying to stop me from getting it. Brazen started to smirk. He replied, this must be a real important medallion. Does it have powers or something? Gray Wolf said yes it does, and everybody on planet earth has the power to turn into an animal. I turn into an Alaskan Gray Wolf. Tauro said I turn into a bull. Brazen said I think you guys are on some serious drugs. Tauro said Amigo, I don't do drugs. Brazen asked what's in it for me.

Gray Wolf said I tell you what, I'll challenge you to a duel. If I win, you come with us, if I lose, we'll leave.

Brazen asked are you serious. Gray Wolf said yeah, we'll leave immediately if I lose. Brazen smiled. He said let's do it.

Tauro stepped back. Gray Wolf and Brazen faced each other. Brazen rushed Gray Wolf with punches. Gray Wolf dodged them and hit Brazen with combination punches. Brazen started blocking his punches and getting his licks in. Brazen threw ice from his hands and froze Gray Wolf's feet. Brazen looked at his hands and realized that he really did have powers. Gray Wolf threw lightning from his hands at his feet and melted the ice. As Gray Wolf ran towards Brazen, he let out a roar and turned into a Polar Bear. He was solid white with black eyes, black nose, black claws and paws. His height and weight seemed impossible for anybody to defeat him. Gray Wolf let out a roar and turned into his Alaskan Gray Wolf form. He growled and showed his teeth as Brazen did the same. He rushed in trying to throw punches. Brazen gave Gray Wolf a powerful kick to the chest knocking him off of his feet. He rushed at Gray Wolf, but was tripped down on one knee. Gray Wolf jumped on Brazen and was punching him until he turned back human. Gray Wolf turned back human, but he still had Brazen pinned down in the snow. Gray Wolf said so, you're coming with us? Brazen said yeah, a deal is a deal, but you know

I let you win because I can't believe I turned into an animal. Gray Wolf smiled, saying yeah right.

Gray Wolf let Brazen up out of the snow. When Brazen is in his human form he can be somewhat of a comedian. When he's in his animal form he can be very serious with great strength.

Gray Wolf asked Brazen, now let me ask you, do you know any other fighters. Brazen thought for a second.

He said yeah, matter of fact I do, but it's a woman. Her name is Sheryl. Tauro said whoa! A woman.

Gray Wolf said where could we locate her. Brazen said she's always downtown by the Arlington hotel.

Gray Wolf said that's Ahshitaw territory. Do you think she would join us? Brazen said I don't know, we can try, but let me warn you, she's a thief. She'll steal your socks of your feet while you're wearing them. She's like a female thug. Gray Wolf and Tauro looked at each other. Gray Wolf said well let's see if she'll join us.

Brazen said well let's go and see if we can find her. Tauro said you better hope we can make it down this icy hill.

Brazen said we'll make it. They all got in the van, going downtown to meet the female fighter named Sheryl.

Chapter 5

SHERYL

Downtown in front of the Arlington hotel, there's a medium height, white female crossing the street to the store.

She's kind of skinny. She has short blonde hair and blue eyes. Some of her hair on the left side of her head comes over her left eye. She does this to make people think she's shy. She has on a dark blue shirt with yellow designs in it.

She has on yellow pants with some yellow ballerina looking shoes on. She's smoking a half of cigarette.

As soon as she crossed the street, she threw the cigarette down and entered the store called Richie's place.

When she walked in, there's another white female in there with a long sleeve, light pink shirt with dark pink pants on sitting down to the right. She has brown eyes with brown hair that comes above her eyelids. The back of her hair comes to her neck. She has an expression on her face like she's serious about something. She has red lip stick and stiletto shoes on. The woman with short blonde hair who entered the store didn't see the woman in pink. She walked up to the counter and talked to the clerk with her soft voice. She said hello sir, how are you.

The clerk said hello Sheryl, how's your day? She said it's going good so far. Sheryl looked at the cash register.

She said to the clerk, sir could you give me change for a ten-dollar bill? I need a five and five ones.

The clerk said sure I can. As he opened the cash register, Sheryl started a different conversation with him. Behind the clerk was a picture of him with a woman and a little girl. Sheryl asked about the picture.

She said sir that picture behind you, is that your wife and daughter? The clerk turned around. He said yes, that's my wife and little girl.

He started to explain that they shot the picture in Hawaii and how they had fun over there. When the clerk turned back around to face Sheryl, she was gone. The clerk thought that was strange. He looked down at the cash register and noticed all his money was gone. He yelled, "Oh my God!" All my money is gone! The woman in the back dressed in pink heard the clerk yelling about how his money was gone. She stood up and asked, did you say her name was Sheryl? The clerk said yes.

The lady in pink said I know her, and walked out the door after Sheryl. She walked to her right and saw Sheryl walking down the alley next to the store. The lady in pink followed her. As Sheryl was walking, she was counting the money she just stole. She started talking to herself, saying what a sucker. That guy wasn't paying attention at all. As she was walking and talking to herself, she heard a voice behind her from the lady in pink. She said to Sheryl, you know that's a real shame. That poor man works and support his family, and you came along and stole his money. I hate thieves. Sheryl stopped and turned around. She looked and recognized who it was.

She said Catherine! Is that your name? The lady in pink said yes, that's my name. You stole my boyfriend in High School, now you stealing from people out of stores. Sheryl said so what, why are you worried about it?

Catherine said that guy is a friend of mine, and I don't like when people steal from my friends.

Sheryl said well get new friends. Catherine said you have two choices. One, either give my friend his money back or two, join the Ahshitaw tribe. Sheryl said how about three, neither one. I'm not giving him his money back and I'm not joining a gang with you. Catherine said the Ahshitaw tribe is not a gang. We're warriors.

Sheryl said well whatever it is, I'm not joining nothing with you. Catherine walked closer to Sheryl as she puts her money in her pocket. Catherine said remember, you brought this on yourself. Sheryl said I'm ready. I'm not scared. Catherine said so be it.

Catherine and Sheryl faced each other for about two seconds. Then Catherine rushed Sheryl throwing punches. Sheryl dodged them, but threw punches back. She did a fast shadow kick. She slid off one-foot and struck Catherine.

Sheryl was focused as she was fighting because she wanted to win. Catherine counter attacked and was hitting Sheryl back.

All of a sudden, Catherine let out a scream. She turned into a Cougar. She had yellow eyes, long claws and paws with a long tail. Sheryl let out a scream and turned into a Cheetah. She had maroon looking eyes and spots all over her body including on her tail. They looked at each other and hissed like cats do. Catherine started talking.

She said get ready to eat dirt. Sheryl said well come with it then.

Catherine charged at Sheryl letting out her Cougar roar. She fought viciously. Sheryl was a Cheetah. She was naturally faster. Catherine didn't stand a chance. Sheryl punched and kicked for about ten seconds until she got Catherine tired and knocking her to the ground. When Catherine hit the ground, she turned back human. Sheryl turned human, and was surprised by how she turned into an animal. Catherine got off the ground. She looked and saw Gray Wolf, Tauro, and Brazen walking behind Sheryl. Catherine said I see you have company. I'll see you again. Catherine ran off. Sheryl is still dazed, but she came to and talked to herself again. She said what company is she talking about. Gray Wolf interrupted and said she's probably talking about us. Sheryl turned around and faced Gray Wolf, Tauro, and Brazen as she is in her fighting stance. She asked who are you. Gray Wolf introduced himself. He said my name is Gray Wolf. I'm from the Kwawpaw tribe. We come in peace. Sheryl looked to her right and saw Brazen. She put her fist down. She asked him, what are you doing here. Have you been dodging bullets lately? Brazen said no, not lately. She looked at Gray Wolf and asked, how do you know me. What do you want?

Gray Wolf said through Brazen. He said he knew you. I hear you are a fighter. Sheryl said I do o.k. for myself.

Gray Wolf said that's good. I see that you turned into a Cheetah. She said yes, I did. Can you explain to me why did that happen? Gray Wolf said yes, my father medallion was snatched off his neck after he was killed. Earth is now cursed with animal instincts because of it. Everybody on earth has the power to turn into an animal when they're angered. Sheryl said, really! All because of a necklace with a medallion on it. So how can you stop this from happening. Gray Wolf said the medallion has to be retrieved by me in two days or we'll be cursed forever.

Sheryl said oh my God! Gray Wolf said the lady you were fighting; did she say anything to you about the Ahshitaw tribe? Sheryl said yes, she asked me to join her in it. Gray Wolf looked surprised. Gray Wolf said she did! What's her name? She's going to come back. Next time she might have more fighters with her. Why don't you join us?

Sheryl said her name is Catherine. I don't know about joining. She reached in her pocket and noticed that her money was gone.

Sheryl said she took my money. Gray Wolf said come with us and maybe we can get it back.

Sheryl thought about it for a second. She said ok I will join you. Tauro said welcome senorita.

Gray Wolf asked Sheryl, do you know any more fighters? She said yes, I do. He's down the street passing out some fliers. He's looking for somebody to. His name is Panthar. I hear he's a weapons expert, and have some nice kickboxing skills. Brazen said If he's a kickboxer, we need to definitely recruit somebody like that.

Gray Wolf said let's see if he'll join us.

Gray Wolf, Tauro, Brazen, and Sheryl went down the street to try to recruit the fighter name Panthar.

Chapter 6

PANTHAR

Just twelve buildings down from Sheryl, was an African American male passing out fliers to everyone that passed him. He has brown eyes with a full goatee. He has on a black beret cap tilted to the right. A black leather jacket that comes down to his knees. Underneath his jacket, he has on a light blue turtle neck shirt, black pants and black leather shoes on. On the flier is a picture of another African American male with a red, black, and green toboggan stretch hat on. The name under the picture was Guerilla. There's a phone number under it to call to get him off the streets. As he was running low on fliers, a deep voice behind him started talking to him.

He said well, well, well, if it isn't the little revolutionary. Panthar looked over and saw who it was. He threw the fliers down. It was the person he was looking for on the flier. Panthar said Guerilla! Do you think you're going to get away with what you've done? Guerilla said I already have.

Guerilla represented the colors of the African flag on his toboggan stretch hat. Red, black, and green. He was muscular and stocky. On the front and back of his black shirt was the continent of Africa, also in red, black, and green colors with a yellow outline. He was a little lighter complexioned than Panthar. He had brown eyes with a thin beard connected to his full goatee. He had the initial of a capital G on his right lower arm.

He had on black gloves, black pants with black boots on. He's a guerilla fighter that uses booby traps and surprise attacks. He's considered a very dangerous person. If you're not another guerilla fighter, he's not your friend.

He escaped death row for the murder of a revolutionary. One of Panthar friends. After earth was cursed with animal instincts, he fought with the guards that were trying to put him to death.

He turned into a Gorilla and broke out of prison. He has a deep hatred for all revolutionaries. He's a street fighter and uses his street fighting skills to defeat his enemies. The revolutionaries and guerillas have been fighting since the late 1960's. The revolutionaries fought for injustice against the police. They were getting respect. The Guerillas became jealous and went to war with them trying to destroy all revolutionaries. Guerilla said to Panthar, So, you're looking for me? You're only looking for trouble. Panthar talked with anger. He said No! You're looking for trouble. I know you killed my friend. He was found hung upside down by his feet with an ice pick in his heart. Only Guerillas kill like that. Guerilla started laughing and replied, Yeah, I guess that's our message to the revolutionaries.

Panthar said you think it's funny. I'm a handle you myself. Guerilla said You can try, but if I win, I'm going to end you. The only way I won't, you'll have to join me in the Ahshitaw tribe. Panthar said I'm not joining you.

Guerilla said o.k. it was your choice. Panthar and Guerilla faced each other to fight.

Guerilla rushed in and threw punches. Panthar put his guards up and kicked Guerilla in the stomach. After he was wounded, Panthar grabbed him by his shoulders and started kneeing him on the left and right side of his ribs. Guerilla counter attacked and hit Panthar in the face and pushed him. Guerilla grabbed Panthar around the waist as they both hit the ground. They punched each other while they were on the ground. Panthar let out a roar and turned into a Black Panther. He was solid black and muscular. He has bright yellow eyes, razor sharp teeth, white claws, white paws, and a tail. Guerilla let out a roar and turned into a Gorilla. He's muscular with dark orange eyes. His arms are longer than his feet. When he's in his Gorilla animal form, he's an acrobatic fighter. He uses his feet like hands. Panthar and Guerilla glared at each other. Guerilla said get ready to meet your maker.

Panthar replied, maybe you're about to meet yours.

Guerilla started beating on his chest and rushed in. Panthar hissed like a cat as his ears folded back on his head because he was getting ready to strike. He jumped over Guerilla head and started hitting him. Since he was a cat, he was faster. Guerilla was fast and he had more strength. They hit each other back and forth. When ten seconds was up, Panthar turned back human. He's confused because this the first time he turned into an animal. He held his hands out. He said to himself, what just happened? I turned into a Black Panther. As he was talking to himself, Guerilla ran towards him.

Panthar reached under his jacket and pulled out a pistol grip pump shot gun. He cocked it and fired at Guerilla, "BOOM", hitting him in the chest and knocked him off of his feet. When Guerilla hit the ground, he turned back human. He got up and started talking. He said, All! You and your weak weapons.

Panthar said It can't be too weak, it knocked you on your back.

Guerilla looked over Panthar shoulder and saw a police car coming their way. He thought it was coming for them.

He said to Panthar, I'm a see you again, you little punk. Next time I'm going to destroy you.

Panthar said forget next time, do it now! Guerilla ran off through car traffic and disappeared.

Panthar tried to chase him, but Gray Wolf interrupted. He said to Panthar, Excuse me! Wait a minute!

Panthar turned around and saw Gray Wolf, Tauro, Brazen, and Sheryl. He asked, who are you? What do you want?

Gray Wolf said I'm from the Kwawpaw tribe. Panthar said what is this Kwawpaw and Ahshitaw stuff?

Gray Wolf asked how did you know about the Ahshitaw tribe. Panthar asked did you see that dude I was just fighting. Gray Wolf said yes, I did. Panthar said he wanted me to join an Ahshitaw tribe with him. I told him I wasn't joining. Gray Wolf said the leader of the Ahshitaw tribe name is Redd Lion. He snatched off my father's necklace and the medallion cursed earth with animal instincts. That's why we turn into animals. What was the guy name you were fighting? Panthar said his name is Guerilla. He's a dangerous dude. He needs to be off the streets. He killed one of my friends in prison.

Gray Wolf said that's the third fighter I've heard of from the Ahshitaw tribe. I ran into one name Tommy. Sheryl fought somebody name Catherine. Now you fought somebody name Guerilla. There's no telling how many other fighters Redd Lion has recruited. Panthar said well Guerilla need to be dealt with for real. I don't know how to get him. Gray Wolf said why don't you come with us, and maybe we can help you. If he's with Redd Lion, you're going to see him again. Panthar said you know what, it's a deal. I'll come with you. I'm a get him for what he's done. Gray Wolf said o.k. that's great. Now it's five of us. I have a question; do you know any more fighters?

Panthar said yeah, he has his own restaurant around the corner. His name is Min Cheng. He's from China. He's a martial arts fighter, plus he's good with electronics.

Gray Wolf said let's go talk to him. Maybe we can recruit him. Panthar said I'm ready, let's go.

Panthar looked and spoke to Sheryl. He said hey, what's up, how have you been? She replied I've been o.k.

Brazen asked, can you teach me some of them kickboxing moves? Panthar said yeah, maybe later.

Tauro spoke to Panthar. He said, what's up amigo? Panthar said what's up man, what's your name? Tauro told him. Panthar shook his hand. Gray Wolf said o.k. everybody, let's go. Gray Wolf, Tauro, Brazen, Sheryl, and Panthar went around the corner to try to recruit the fighter name Min Cheng.

Chapter 7

MIN CHENG

Around the corner on Broadway Street is restaurant PHT owned by Min Cheng. The rush hour is over. All the customers left for the day. Min Cheng was cleaning up the restaurant. He has spiked hair, slanted light brown eyes and no facial hair. He's dressed in a purple and white Kung Fu suit. He has white socks with purple and white shoes on. There's a white towel around his waist that he uses to wipe off the tables with.

After he wiped off the last table, he fixed him a plate of food to eat. He's getting ready to eat rice with chicken and broccoli on top of it. He sat down at a table with chop sticks in his hand. He grabbed a piece of chicken with them and getting ready to put a piece of it in his mouth when suddenly he heard a voice speaking to him from behind. The guy has long hair with an orange sweat band in front of his hair. He has slanted brown eyes with a Fu Manchu mustache and goatee. He has on an orange ninja suit with a sword on his back. He has on black ninja boots that comes to his knees. He said to Min Cheng, hello, this is a very nice restaurant.

Min Cheng put the chop sticks down, jumped up and asked, who are you? What are you doing here?

The guy in the orange ninja suit said my name is Tarashi. I'm second in command of the Ahshitaw tribe as he walked closer. Min Cheng pulled the towel off from around his waist. He asked Tarashi, what is the Ahshitaw tribe?

Tarashi said It's a team of warriors that's getting ready to take over land and businesses.

Min Cheng replied, if you think you're going to take over this business, you have another thing coming.

Tarashi started laughing. He stopped and said join me in the Ahshitaw tribe and I won't take your business.

Min Cheng said I'm not joining you and you're not taking my business. He looked at Tarashi's clothing.

He said wait a minute, you're a ninja. You got to be from Japan.

Tarashi said yeah, I'm one of Japan's deadliest ninjas. I'm master of tiger style fighting.

Tarashi looked at Min Cheng's suit. He said so you're from China huh? The only fighters from China in purple Kung Fu suits, are the Purple Heart Triads. Min Cheng said yes, I'm a part of the Purple Heart Triads, now leave my restaurant. I don't like ninjas. Tarashi replied, Is that so? Well ninjas don't like you either. Make me leave.

Min Cheng said your wish is my command. He and Tarashi got into their fighting stance, facing each other.

Tarashi charged and threw punches. Min Cheng dodged them. Tarashi threw a round house kick as Min Cheng duck and did a sweep kick and knocked Tarashi off of his feet. Tarashi quickly got up and threw a straight kick to Min Cheng chest, but barely faded him. Min Cheng punched Tarashi in the face twice and did a round house kick and struck him in the face again. Min Cheng was just as fast with his feet as he was with his hands. Tarashi had the same speed. They punched and kicked each other repeatedly. Suddenly Tarashi went into his animal rage. He threw his hands to the side and hollered. He changed into a Tiger. He had yellowish eyes, sharp teeth, and stripes over his whole body, a tail, white sharp claws, and paws. He opened his mouth and let out a ferocious roar. Min Cheng let out a roar and turned into a

Purple Dragon. He had solid white eyes, bat looking wings, black claws, and paws. Tarashi spoke to Min Cheng. He said may you rest in peace. This is your last day on earth.

Min Cheng said I don't think so.

Tarashi charged in. Min Cheng flapped his wings, flew towards Tarashi and grabbed him by the waist. They both was in the air. They knocked over tables that were in the restaurant. They put up a big fight on one another for about ten seconds. Before Tarashi turned back human, Min Cheng stepped back, opened his mouth and let out a long flame of fire towards Tarashi. After the flame went away, Tarashi turned back human. Min Cheng turned human and was shocked that he turned into a Purple Dragon. Tarashi looked over and saw Gray Wolf, Tauro, Brazen, Sheryl, and Panthar entering the restaurant. He assumed they were coming to help Min Cheng. Tarashi said oh, you got reinforcements coming in. I'm going to catch you on the rebound. Min Cheng asked, what reinforcements are you talking about? Min Cheng ran and did a flying kick.

Tarashi threw a pill on the floor that burst into smoke. When Min Cheng jumped through it trying to kick him, he had disappeared. Min Cheng was in his fighting stance. He started talking to himself. He said what is this world coming to? I turned into a Dragon. Gray Wolf interrupted. He said yeah, it's because of my father's medallion.

Min Cheng turned around to face Gray Wolf, Tauro, Brazen, Sheryl, and Panthar because he didn't know what to expect. He was still in his fighting stance. Gray Wolf held his right hand out and said, we come in peace. I want to talk to you for a minute. Min Cheng looked at Panthar as he nodded his head yes. Min Cheng let his guards down.

He asked, what do you want to talk about? Gray Wolf said we were looking through the window and watching the person you were fighting. Min Cheng said, really! Sheryl said yeah really! Dude you beat him down.

Min Cheng said thank you. I had to. Gray Wolf asked did you get the guy name you were fighting.

Min Cheng said yes, he said his name was Tarashi. He said he was second in command in some Ahshitaw tribe.

Gray Wolf asked, he said he was second in command? Min Cheng said yes, and he asked me to join him, but I told him I wasn't. Gray Wolf said well I'm from the Kwawpaw tribe. If he said he's second in command in the Ahshitaw tribe, then he know exactly where Redd Lion is and know how to get to him. Min Cheng asked who's Redd Lion?

Gray Wolf said he's the leader of the Ahshitaw tribe now. He's the reason why we turn into animals.

Min Cheng asked why do we turn into animals. Gray Wolf said it's because of my father's medallion. Redd Lion snatched it off my father's neck when he was killed. Now earth is cursed with animal instincts. I need to get it back by tomorrow or we're going to turn into animals forever. Min Cheng asked do you need me to come with you and help? That guy I fought is a ninja. He's a tiger style fighter. I'll challenge and probably beat him. I'm a member of the Purple Heart Triads. I won't rest until he's defeated. Gray Wolf said yeah, that's great. We can give his fighters a good fight to get Redd Lion's attention. Min Cheng said o.k. I'll come with you. That guy has a sword on his back. I'll bring my nun chucks and stars with me. Gray Wolf asked what are stars. Min Cheng said they're knives, but are in the shape of stars. Panthar asked you mean you could hold that guy off with Nun Chucks.

Min Cheng said yes, I done it before. Panthar asked so what's the next move. Gray Wolf said we need to go and get Tauro's van to drive around and look for Redd Lion's fighters to find out where he's at.

Min Cheng said wait, I have my Suburban truck behind my restaurant. We can use that.

Tauro said good amigo, I didn't want to walk back up the street to get my van any way.

Brazen said well let's do it. I'm ready.

Min Cheng said you know what, I almost forgot. Earlier there was a rapper down at the convenient store selling his c.ds. He said somebody from the Ahshitaw tribe tried to recruit him. He said his name was Black Male.

Gray Wolf said well let's go and see if he's still down there. We can ask who tried to recruit him and possibly we can get him to join us. Min Cheng said let me grab my weapons, lock my restaurant up, and we can drive down to see him if he's still there. Gray Wolf said o.k. He, Tauro, Brazen, Sheryl, Panthar, and Min Cheng left the restaurant. They got in the Suburban and went down to the convenient store to meet the guy name Black Male. Gray Wolf was anxious to see who was trying to recruit him in the Ahshitaw tribe.

Chapter 8

NEUTRAL FIGHTERS

In front of the convenient store is an African American male name Black Male with c.ds in his hand. Every time somebody come to the store, he asked them to buy his c.d. He has a bald fade haircut, brown eyes, a mustache and goatee that's not connected.

He has on a white t-shirt with the initials of B.O.S.S in front of it. He has on black pants with white shoes on. Suddenly an older white male walked up and was looking at the c.ds in Black Male hand. The older white male had to be in his late 40's or early 50's. He had on a light brown fedora hat with a dark brown stripe across it.

He had brown eyes with a menacing look and a full beard. He had on a long sleeve maroon shirt, blue overalls, and yellow boots on. He talks with a very country accent. Black Male saw him and spoke. He said, what's up man? Do you want to check out one of my c.ds? The old man said, no, I don't listen to that rap stuff. Why are you down here in front of this store like this? Black Male said it's called hustling. The old man said go get you a job.

Black Male said I got one. What's your name? Where are you from? You're country. The old man said the name is Farmer Ed, I'm from Mississippi. Black Male said Farmer Ed. You're name fit because you look like you're from a farm. Farmer Ed asked are you making fun of me? Black Male said yeah you can say that. If you're not buying a c.d. what do you want? Farmer Ed said I want a percentage of your earnings if you're selling anything in front of this store. Black Male said you don't own this store. I'm not giving you nothing.

Farmer Ed said Well give me half of your c.ds, I'll sale them and make a profit. Black Male said I'm not giving you my c.ds, and if you try to take them, we're going to have a real problem. Farmer Ed said well I guess we're going to have a problem because I'm taking your c.ds. Farmer Ed reached and tried to take Black Male c.ds. and got pushed. Farmer Ed said if this is what you want, I'm about to whoop your butt boy!

Black Male put his c.ds down. He replied, I'm not your boy.
O.K. try it.

Black Male and Farmer Ed faced each other. Farmer Ed rushed
in, threw punches and kicks, but Black Male dodged them. Black
Male punched Farmer Ed with two left and right blows to the
face. Farmer Ed got more violent. He and Black Male punched
and kicked each other until Farmer Ed went into animal rage.

He turned into a Rooster. He had red and black eyes, a big
yellow beak, and feathers all over his body that matched the colors
of his clothes. He had maroon feathers from his head to his waist.
He had blue feathers from his waist to his knees, and yellow knees
to his feet with big white paws with a bushy red feather as a tail.
Black Male went into animal rage and turned into a Rottweiler
dog. He was muscular from his head to feet. His face was black,
with brown eyes and two brown dots above both of his eyes,
and under his chin was brown. His body was black and from his
elbow to hands was brown with black claws. His legs were black,
but from his knees to feet was brown with black paws. He and
Farmer Ed talked to each other. Farmer Ed said I told you I'm
taking your c.ds.

Black Male said well try to take them. Farmer Ed said I will.

Farmer Ed ran towards Black Male at full speed. Black Male started growling and showing his teeth. Farmer Ed jumped in the air trying to kick. Black Male blocked it, and counter attacked and started throwing punches and hitting Farmer Ed in the face. Black Male fought viciously. He was meaner. He opened his mouth and bit Farmer Ed under his neck. Farmer Ed hollered like Roosters do. He punched Black Male but it didn't seem like he fazed him. Black Male threw four big left and right punches at Farmer Ed and knocked him down. When he fell, he was knocked out cold as he turned back human. Black Male was still in his animal form. He walked up to Farmer Ed, bent down and grabbed him by his shirt. He growled as if he was going to bite him.

He was interrupted by Gray Wolf as he said, "Excuse me!"

When Black Male heard Gray Wolf's voice, he turned back human. He let go of Farmer Ed's shirt and stood up to face Gray Wolf, Tauro, Brazen, Sheryl, Panthar, and Min Cheng.

Black Male said what's up man. Gray Wolf asked, how are you? He introduced himself and said he was from the Kwawpaw tribe.

Black Male said what's going on, did you see me turn into a dog. I turned into a Rottweiler.

Gray Wolf said yeah, it's because of my father's medallion. Earth is cursed with animal instincts because of it. A guy name Redd Lion is responsible for what's happening. Black Male said did you say Redd Lion? I heard of him. He killed a man because he wouldn't join him in a gang or something.

Gray Wolf asked, he did? Do you mean the Ahshitaw tribe? Black Male said yeah, it's in today's newspaper. I got it right here. Black Male took the newspaper out of his back pocket to give it to Gray Wolf. He grabbed the newspaper to read.

On the front page, it says a local man was killed by an Indian fighter. It describes an Indian with a Mohawk with war paint on his face, dressed in red clothing, that turned into a lion that killed a man because he wouldn't join his tribe. Gray Wolf folded the newspaper and gave it back to Black Male. He said oh my God! It's him! We got to get him off the streets. He killed that man the same day he took my father's medallion from him.

Tauro asked where do we look amigo. Gray Wolf said I don't know. Black Male said I heard he's recruiting fighters. Come to think about it, somebody came to me this morning dressed in green camouflage clothing, asking me did I want to join some Ahshitaw tribe. He said his name was Cajun. He's tall and he talks with a Cajun accent. He hangs around at the Cajun Boilers restaurant on Albert Pike. I think he's from the military.

Black Male looked and pointed at Brazen. He said he's his height. Brazen said If he's my height, I'll challenge him.

Sheryl said you'll challenge anybody. Brazen said I sure will. Gray Wolf asked Black Male, would you like to join us.

Black Male said I can't. I got money to collect. I'm neutral right now. I do rap music. I'm selling my new album now. Min Cheng looked at Farmer Ed on the ground. He asked Gray Wolf, what about him.

Black Male said he never told me he was with any gang or tribe. He might be neutral to. He tries to extort money from people. It doesn't work with me. Gray Wolf said thanks for the information. We got to find this Cajun guy and find out where Redd Lion is. Black Male said o.k. be careful, I hear Redd Lion throws fireballs out of his hands when he's human. When he turns into a lion, he's going to be hard to beat. Gray Wolf said I got to try. I got to get that medallion back. Black Male said do what you got to do. Gray Wolf said I will. Let me know if you need anything. Black Male said o.k. I will. Panthar stepped forward and asked Black Male, what's the name of your c.d. and how much is it. Black Male said "Diary of a Lyricist", and they're $10. You should check out one.

Panthar reached in his pocket and pulled out a 10 dollar bill and gave it to Black Male. Panthar was given a c.d. for his $10. Black Male said thanks, you'll like it. Panthar said o.k. I'll check it out. Gray Wolf said see you around.

Black Male said o.k. I'm a leave before the police show up, and walked off. Gray Wolf looked up at the sky and noticing that the clouds were getting darker. Gray Wolf looked up at the sky and noticed that the clouds are getting darker. He asked what time is it. Panthar said 6:30 P.M. Gray Wolf said we got to hurry up and get that medallion back. Gray Wolf, Tauro, Brazen, Sheryl, Panthar, and Min Cheng got into the Suburban to go on Albert Pike to the Cajun Boilers restaurant to find the fighter name Cajun.

Chapter 9

BRAZEN VS. CAJUN

Gray Wolf and the Kwawpaw fighters made it to Albert Pike on their way to the Cajun Boilers restaurant. In the front seat, Min Cheng was driving, Sheryl was in the middle and Gray Wolf was on the far right. In the back seat, Panthar was on the far left, Tauro was in the middle, and Brazen was on the far right. As they were riding, Gray Wolf started giving advice to everybody.

He said for now on, before or after you challenge someone, announce to them that you're a Kwawpaw fighter. The message will get to Redd Lion faster. Brazen said I hear you. Sheryl said I be glad when I catch up with Catherine. She took my money. Panthar said Sheryl, you don't forget nothing do you? She said nope. Tauro said If she took my money, I would want it to. Gray Wolf said we'll find her, but we need to catch up with that ninja

Min Cheng was fighting. He knows exactly how to reach Redd Lion. Min Cheng said I really need to catch up with him. He's going to give me my respect.

Gray Wolf said you'll get it.

They pulled up at the Cajun Boilers restaurant. As everybody got out of the Suburban, Gray Wolf looked towards the restaurant and saw a tall white male dressed in green camouflage clothing walking behind the restaurant to a boat because there's a lake behind Cajun Boilers. Gray Wolf turned around and talked to everybody. He said look! It's a guy in camouflage like Black Male described. Brazen asked do you think it's him. Gray Wolf said I don't know, but we're going to find out.

Gray Wolf and the Kwawpaw fighters went to speak to the guy in camouflage. Gray Wolf stepped forward and spoke.

He said hello, what's your name? The man in camouflage turned around and acknowledged him. He asked, Why? Who wants to know? Brazen said well he do talk with a Cajun accent. The man in camouflage gave Gray Wolf a weird look like if he had met him before. Gray Wolf said I was just asking. The man in camouflage said my name is Cajun. Brazen said yep, that's him.

Cajun was a tall white male. He stood over 6 foot tall. He had on a green cowboy hat with the left side turned up like an Australian hunter. It had a yellow stripe across it. The hair on his eyebrows and mustache was red. He had green eyes. He looked like if he was Irish.

His jacket and pants were green, black, and yellow camouflage colors. He had his jacket unbuttoned. He had on a green shirt with silver military dog tags around his neck with green boots with yellow shoelaces. Gray Wolf said I heard of you.

Cajun said by your description, I heard of you to. Your Gray Wolf of the Kwawpaw tribe, right? Gray Wolf and the Kwawpaw fighters looked at each other. Gray Wolf said yes, I am. How did you know? Cajun said because you got into a scuffle with one of my friends. His name is Tommy. Gray Wolf said yeah that's right! So, you working with Redd Lion as well? Where is he? Cajun said I'm not telling you. Brazen said yeah, you're going to tell us, or we'll beat the truth out of you.

Cajun said you can try, but you won't get far. Do I have to fight all six of you? Brazen said no, I'll fight you. If I win, you tell us where Redd Lion and all of his fighters are. Cajun looked down at the ground for a second. He looked back and said o.k. It's a deal.

Brazen looked back at Gray Wolf and said I don't like the way he said that. Gray Wolf said me either.

Brazen signaled to Gray Wolf and everybody to stay back. He looked at Cajun and said I'm ready. Cajun said me to.

Brazen and Cajun faced each other.

Cajun charged at full speed. Brazen threw ice from his hands to the ground and freezing it. When Cajun ran across it, he slipped and fell. Brazen jumped in the air and struck Cajun in the face. He grabbed Brazen by the shoulders and threw him to the side. They both got up to face each other again. Cajun spit green slime out of his mouth at Brazen. He ducked and charged in as they continue to hit each other. All of a sudden, Cajun went into his animal rage and turned into an Alligator.

He had snake looking eyes, and a long mouth full of sharp teeth. He was muscular with black claws. He had a long tail with seem to be spikes on it with black paws. Brazen went into his animal rage and turned into his Polar Bear animal form.

Cajun started talking to him. He said you must be crazy if you think you're going to win this. Brazen said well I guess I must be crazy.

He ran toward Cajun as he swung his tail. Brazen jumped over it and gave Cajun a kick to the chest. He was knocked down but got up quickly. Cajun fought very viciously. He even threw bite attacks, but somehow Brazen dodged them. He attacked Brazen as they punched and kicked each other. As Cajun was punched with a final blow to the face, he turned back human, as so did Brazen. He said to Cajun, you need more fighting skills lizard man. Cajun said how about you try this.

He reached under his jacket and pulled out a grenade. He pulled out the pin and slid it towards his feet. Brazen turned around and ran toward Gray Wolf and the Kwawpaw fighters. Everybody was standing in front of Sheryl. She didn't see Cajun throw the grenade. She broke through everybody trying to chase Cajun as Gray Wolf yelled, NO!

He grabbed Sheryl by the waist, turning her around, as they and everybody hit the ground. The grenade exploded, KABOOM! Seconds later, everybody got up as Cajun jumped in a boat behind the restaurant and rode off. Gray Wolf helped Sheryl up off of the ground. When he did, she fell in love with him instantly. He started talking to her.

He said I'm sorry if I hurt you. Sheryl said no, you saved my life, thank you. Brazen walked over. He said that fool lied to us, he was supposed to tell us where Redd Lion and his fighters were. Panthar said he threw that grenade; he was trying to kill us. Tauro said now it's serious. They want to play for keeps; we're going to do the same thing.

Min Cheng looked over where Brazen and Cajun were fighting and saw a piece of paper and silver military dog tags. He walked over and grabbed them. He opened the piece of paper and saw it was a map with names on it.

Min Cheng said look at this, It's a map and that guy dog tags. He gave it to Gray Wolf. He looked at the map and threw the dog tags to Brazen, saying here's a souvenir. Brazen said well I'm a see if he'll come back for these.

Gray Wolf said here are all the names of everybody in the Ahshitaw tribe. Tommy, Catherine, Guerilla, Tarashi, and Cajun. Their names are in front of businesses. Why isn't Redd Lion not on it? Min Cheng said he got them doing his dirty work.

Gray Wolf said the next person on the list is Tommy. He's going to try to take over a bar business.

Gray Wolf looked at Tauro. He said remember that bald head guy that walked through your land when I met you?

Tauro said yeah, I remember him. Gray Wolf said he's next on the list. I know where he's going to be. He's going to be at the bar over on Convention Blvd.

Tauro said he must be an alcoholic, if he's taking over a bar. Well we need to go and get him.

Gray Wolf said I'm ready.

Everybody walked towards Min Cheng Suburban to go to the bar where Tommy is going to be. As they were riding, Sheryl grabbed Gray Wolf's hand as if they were in a relationship. She smiled and acted like she wanted to kiss him.

Chapter 10

TAURO VS. TOMMY

Back across town on Convention Blvd at the bar on the corner, many people are in their drinking, shooting pool, talking loudly, and eating. As soon as Tommy walked in, everybody looked up and had stopped what they were doing. Tommy walked over and unplugged the jukebox. He walked up to the woman behind the bar and started talking to her. He asked, who is the owner of the bar? The clerk said his name is Bill, but he's not here. He will be in later. Why? Tommy said I want this bar. The clerk asked what do you mean you want this bar? How do you know it's for sale? Tommy said I didn't know it was for sale. I'm taking it. The clerk started looking at Tommy funny. The clerk asked how are you going to take it. Tommy said if he doesn't sale it to me, I'll challenge him to a fight. If I win, I get the bar. The clerk said dude either you're on drugs or you're crazy.

Tommy said neither one. I work for Redd Lion of the Ahshitaw tribe, and he's taking over businesses.

The clerk said well he or you are not taking this business, so you might as well leave. Tommy asked who's going to make me leave. Gray Wolf, Tauro, Brazen, Sheryl, Panthar, and Min Cheng walked in the bar.

Gray Wolf walked up to the bar and said, don't worry ma'am, we'll make him leave. Tommy turned around and saw Gray Wolf. He said oh no! Not you again. What are you, a bounty hunter? Gray Wolf said yeah, you can say that. We're hunting all of the Ahshitaw fighters. Tommy asked, what do you mean? Brazen stepped forward and threw Cajun dog tags at his feet. Tommy picked them up to look at. He said these are Cajuns. Where is he?

Brazen said he just got a serious beating. Tauro said now you know what he means about us hunting all of the Ahshitaw fighters. Tommy asked, who are you. Tauro told him his name. He said I'm a Kwawpaw fighter. You trespassed through my land earlier. That's disrespect. Tommy looked at Gray Wolf. He said oh, you got a whole gang of fighters now. Gray Wolf said yeah, I do, now where is Redd Lion? Tommy said he's minding his business and I suggest you mind yours. Gray Wolf said you're going to tell me where he is.

Tommy looked at Sheryl. He said I'll tell you if she gives me her phone number. Sheryl said I'm not giving you nothing. Tauro saw the scar on Tommy jaw. He said hey Scarface! Where is Redd Lion? Tommy got angry.

He said don't call me Scarface! Do you know how I got this scar? Tauro said I don't care how you got it. Where is Redd Lion? Tommy said none of your business! Tauro said come on Scarface, you're wasting our time.

Tommy pointed his finger at Tauro and said If you call me Scarface again, I'm a beat the snot out of you.

Tauro told Gray Wolf and the Kwawpaw fighters to stand back. They all went over by the jukebox.

Tauro turned back around and looked Tommy directly in the eye. He said where is Redd Lion? Scarface!

Tommy said I told you not to call me that again didn't I! He charged at Tauro.

He punched and kicked as Tauro blocked them. Tauro kicked at his knee and started punching Tommy in the face. Tommy counter attacked and started punching back. They both were landing in punches. Suddenly they both went into their animal rage at the same time. Tommy turned into his Warthog animal form. Tauro turned into his bull animal form. They started talking to each other. Tommy said you're going to learn about calling me names.

Tauro said I don't think so, Scarface!

Tommy charged at him. Tauro stuck his head down by Tommy waist. He charged at Tommy with his black horns. Tommy was hit in the ribs and was knocked off of his feet. Tauro and Tommy continued to punch and kick each other. Finally, Tommy turned back human, as so did Tauro as he taunted Tommy. He said I'm a bull. You're a hog. You'll never beat me, Scarface. Tommy charged Tauro. He said I told you not to call me that!

Tommy ran to Tauro and threw punches. Tauro ducked and gave Tommy a strong uppercut and knocked him down. When he fell, Tauro ran to Tommy and grabbed him by his shirt. He asked where is Redd Lion?

Tommy said I'm not telling you nothing. Get away from me.

Tauro was enraged. He punched Tommy with a hard right to the face. Tommy was knocked out cold.

Gray Wolf, Brazen, Sheryl, Panthar, and Min Cheng walked over to Tauro. Gray Wolf said you knocked him out. He'll never tell us where Redd Lion is at now. Tauro said I don't know my own strength. I didn't mean to knock him out. Gray Wolf said well you did because he's asleep. Gray Wolf walked over to the clerk.

He said you don't have to worry about him taking your bar. The clerk said thank You. I'll call the police so they can get him out of here. Gray Wolf said o.k. He reached in his pocket and pulled out the map. He looked up at Sheryl and said guess who's next on the list? Sheryl asked who. Gray Wolf said Catherine. Sheryl said really! Where is she going to be? Gray Wolf said at a clothing store on Malvern Avenue. Sheryl said let's go get her.

Gray Wolf said o.k. I'm ready. Gray Wolf and the Kwawpaw fighters got in Min Cheng Suburban truck to find Catherine.

Chapter 11

SHERYL VS. CATHERINE

Around the corner from the bar on Malvern Avenue is K's Fashion. It's a clothing store owned by an Asian family. Catherine walked up to the door and there was a sign that says will return in 15 minutes. Catherine talked to herself. She said oh great, I have to sit here and wait for somebody to show up.

Beside the K Fashion store is Cash Saver's grocery store. There are benches where you can sit down at. Catherine went over and sat. Minutes have gone by. A white car pulled up in front of K's Fashion. A black Suburban truck pulled up in front of Catherine. For some reason she got a bad feeling about the Suburban. She sensed something wrong. Catherine looked over at K's Fashion and saw an Asian woman and a teenage girl walk up to the door, opened it and went inside. Catherine got up and went over to the store to go in, but she heard a voice behind her.

It said where do you think you're going. Catherine turned around and saw Sheryl, Gray Wolf, Tauro, Brazen, Panthar, and Min Cheng getting out of the Suburban. Catherine said to herself, I knew I had a bad feeling about that truck. She said to Sheryl, I'm going in this store. Why? Sheryl said you mean you're trying to take over this business, right? Catherine walked slowly in front of Sheryl. She asked, who told you that?

Sheryl said nobody told me, but I know that's what you're trying to do. Catherine said what if I am, what are you going to do, stop me? Sheryl replied yes, I am, and I want the money you took out of my pocket.

Catherine laughed and looked at the other fighters behind her. She said so, you have a team of fighters with you trying to stop our process. Sheryl said yeah, that's right. We're going to stop your progress. You're not taking over any businesses, so you might as well leave.

Catherine said you're going to have to make me leave. Sheryl said if that's the way you want it, so be it. Catherine replied, o.k. but I'm not going to be easy on you like the last time. Sheryl said give me all you got; you don't scare me. Sheryl and Catherine got into their fighting stances.

Sheryl rushed in swinging as Catherine block her punches. Sheryl did a side kick and struck her in the ribs. Catherine was wounded. Sheryl hit her in the face. Catherine swung and started hitting Sheryl back.

They punched and kicked each other for ten seconds until suddenly they both went into their animal rage. Sheryl turned into her Cheetah animal form. Catherine turned into her Cougar form. They talked to each other. Sheryl said you're leaving this property. Catherine said I don't think so.

Catherine looked down and saw a brick. She picked it up, cocked her arm back to throw it. Sheryl was looking at what she was doing. She ran at Catherine, picking up speed to 70 mph in an instant. Before Catherine threw the brick, Sheryl was in front of her, punching her in the face. Catherine was knocked down.

Sheryl jumped on top of her, grabbing underneath her throat and held her until they both turned back human.

When they did, Sheryl reached in Catherine pocket and got her money back. Sheryl got off her. She said to Catherine, I got my money back. Catherine said so what, you can have that chump change. Gray Wolf asked Catherine, where is Redd Lion? She asked Gray Wolf, why are you looking for him? Gray Wolf said because he got my father's necklace and medallion. I need it back by tomorrow. Catherine said you really think you're getting that necklace and medallion back by tomorrow. Mankind will be cursed with animal instincts forever, then we're really going to take over businesses and your Kwawpaw territory. Gray Wolf turned to his fighters.

So that was his plan all along. He wanted mankind to be cursed with animal instincts forever. He figures because he turns into a lion that can't nobody beat him; she's going to tell us where he is.

Gray Wolf, Tauro, Brazen, Sheryl, Panthar, and Min Cheng walked toward Catherine. She reached in her pocket and pulled out a pink ball. She threw it at the ground, and it busted with a bright pink light coming from it.

The light lasted for about three seconds. Gray Wolf and the Kwawpaw fighters had no choice but to look away. When their vision came back, Catherine disappeared. Brazen said she's gone. Sheryl said I should have held her down until she told us something. Gray Wolf said It's o.k. we still have the map and there's a couple more fighters that we'll run across. Panthar asked who's next on the map. Gray Wolf pulled out the map for a second. He looked up at Panthar.

Gray Wolf said you're in luck. That person you fought named Guerilla is next. I wonder why they have a jail circled on here.

Panthar looked up. He said they're planning on breaking some Guerilla members out of jail. Gray Wolf asked, you think so?

Panthar said I know so. Trust me; you don't want any more of them on the streets. We have to stop them now.

Gray Wolf said yeah, you're right. Tauro said well let's go Amigo.

Gray Wolf, Tauro, Brazen, Sheryl, Panthar, and Min Cheng got in the Suburban and went to the jail to stop Guerilla from breaking some of his members out of jail.

Chapter 12

PANTHAR VS. GUERILLA

Behind the Hot Springs police department, Guerilla is looking at the cells that was built by brick. He's counting them. When he counted the seventh one, he pulled out six sticks of dynamite that had black tape around them.

He placed it on the cell. He pulled out a lighter and was getting ready to light the stem. Before he could, he heard Panthar's voice saying I wouldn't do that if I was you. Guerilla turned around and saw Panthar, Gray Wolf, Tauro, Brazen, Sheryl, and Min Cheng. Guerilla asked Panthar, what do you want? Panthar said we're stopping you from breaking your members out of jail. Guerilla asked, how did you know I was here? Panthar said we smelled you.

Gray Wolf said you're going to tell us where Redd Lion is. Guerilla said over my dead body. Panthar said well may you rest in peace. Guerilla said so, you have a click of fighters with you. What are you going to do, jump me?

Tauro said we don't have to jump you, but you're going to give us the dynamite. Brazen said that's right.

Guerilla said I'm not giving you nothing. Panthar said yes you are, now hand it over. Guerilla put the dynamite in his front pocket. He said to Panthar, if you want it, then take it. Panthar said o.k. I sure will. Guerilla said I know you got that pump shot gun. Panthar reached under his coat, pulled out his shotgun and gave it to Gray Wolf as he and the rest of the Kwawpaw fighters stepped back.

Panthar and Guerilla stood in front of each other. Panthar charged in and threw punches. Guerilla blocked and dodged them. Panthar was a kickboxer, so he kicked Guerilla in the groins. When Guerilla dropped down on one knee, Panthar punched him in the face. Guerilla grabbed Panthar by his shoulders and threw him to the side.

Panthar quickly got up and charged again. Guerilla blocked his punches, but somehow, got behind him, grabbing Panthar by his neck and twisted it, trying to break it. Panthar got up and went into his animal rage.

He turned into his Black Panther animal form. Guerilla went into his animal rage and turned into his Gorilla animal form. Panthar said It's not easy to beat me. Guerilla said I'm not going to just beat you; I'm going to kill you.

Panthar said o.k. try it. Guerilla rushed in swinging. Panthar dodged his punches. He swung and hit Guerilla in the face six or seven times and one uppercut. As Guerilla flew up in the air, Panthar jumped, attacked, punched, and kicked Guerilla until he hit the ground. When he landed, he turned back human. Panthar came down and landed on top of him. He turned back human. He walked up on Guerilla and took the dynamite out of his pocket. He said I have a feeling we might need this for something, and you won't be breaking any Guerillas out of jail.

Guerilla got up. He said the day is going to come when I bury you. Panthar asked, is that all you do is make threats? You're not going to do nothing, now tell us where Redd Lion is. Guerilla said I'm not telling you nothing, go find him. Panthar said yeah, we will find him, and we're going to stop what y'all are trying to do. Guerilla said we'll see. He pulled out one short stem stick of dynamite out. He lit it and threw it toward Panthar and the rest of the Kwawpaw fighters. Everybody dove for the ground as the dynamite exploded, "KABOOM!" Seconds later, everybody got up. Panthar said we're behind a police station, we got to go. Gray Wolf said you're right.

Min Cheng said let's go!

Gray Wolf and the Kwawpaw fighters ran to the Suburban, got in and left from behind the police station.

As Min Cheng was driving, Panthar got mad. He hit the back seat. "WHOP!" He said that's the second time somebody has threw bombs at us. We need to catch this Redd Lion fool. Gray Wolf said yeah, I know, we're on the right trail. Panthar said Guerilla is a killer. The only reason he's hanging around the Ahshitaw fighters because he's running from the police. If he had a chance, he would fight his own members. Sheryl asked what do we do now.

Gray Wolf pulled out the map and looked. He said guess what, this is the last business on the map. It's the Boys Club. Tauro asked why would they have the Boys Club on a map? Brazen said believe it or not, but it's a major business for kids and grown-ups. Min Cheng said I heard earlier that they're having a fighting competition tonight. Gray Wolf said that guy, Tarashi is going to be there. Min Cheng said that's the Ninja I fought in my restaurant. Gray Wolf said yeah, it sure is. Min Cheng said so, are we going to the Boys Club? Once I make an enemy, I can't rest until he's defeated. Gray Wolf said well, let's go. This time, he's going to tell us where Redd Lion is. Min Cheng said o.k. let's go and get him.

Gray Wolf and the Kwawpaw fighters went to the Boys Club to find Tarashi.

Chapter 13

MIN CHENG VS. TARASHI

At the Boys Club, there are hundreds of people and fighters around. Tarashi walked in as some people looked at him like he was weird. In the boxing ring there was a silver microphone that was hanging down from the ceiling. Tarashi walked in the boxing ring and started talking on the microphone. He said Excuse me! Everybody let me get your attention. All the people and fighters had stopped what they were doing and looked at him.

Tarashi asked, who is the owner of the Boys Club? A big stocky white guy with a receiving hair line in the crowd came forward and said I am. Tarashi asked can you come forward for a minute. I would like to talk to you.

The owner who was a fighter himself, walked up and got in the ring with Tarashi. He asked, yeah, what do you want? Tarashi said I would like to challenge you to a fight for the ownership of the Boys Club. The owner asked Is this a joke. Tarashi said no, it's not. I challenge you. If I win, I get the Boys Club. If you win, I will leave.

The owner looked around and noticed how all the people and fighters was watching and hearing what was being said. Before the owner could answer, he heard a voice behind him saying I'll challenge him. The owner and Tarashi looked over and it was Min Cheng, Gray Wolf, Tauro, Brazen, Sheryl, and Panthar. Min Cheng got in the ring and had a talk with the owner. He said let me challenge him, I can beat him, then you don't have to worry about losing your club. The owner looked over at Tarashi, then looked back at Min Cheng. He said o.k. It's a deal. He looked at Min Cheng and asked what's your name. Then he asked Tarashi's his. They both told him. The owner snatched the microphone out of Tarashi's hand. The owner said ladies and gentlemen, we have two new challengers in the Boys Club. One is Min Cheng and the other is Tarashi. The crowd hollered and cheered. The owner told Min Cheng and Tarashi to shake hands.

Tarashi said I don't want to shake hands. Min Cheng said that's fine with me.

Min Cheng got in one corner and Tarashi got in the other. The owner told them that there are no rules. It's a fight for survival as he left the ring. Min Cheng and Tarashi got in their fighting stances as they got closer to each other.

Tarashi threw punches as Min Cheng blocked them. Tarashi threw a kick to the chest. Min Cheng blocked it as he threw two punches and striking Tarashi in the face. Min Cheng and Tarashi threw punches and roundhouse kicks at each other as Min Cheng got the best of him. Tarashi got angry. He pulled his sword from his back. He said now I'm going to cut you into pieces. Min Cheng pulled his Nun-Chucks from the side of his pants. He swung each stick-on chain from arm to arm. Tarashi didn't no he had them. Min Cheng said you think you're the only one with weapons.

Tarashi said you're no match for me with weapons. Min Cheng said o.k. let's see. The chain between Min Cheng Nun-Chucks were Chinese stainless steel. A sword couldn't cut it.

Tarashi swung his sword back and forth at Min Cheng as he blocked his blade. Tarashi couldn't hit Min Cheng. Finally, Tarashi swung his sword as Min Cheng wrapped his Nun-Chucks around his sword and snatched it out of his hand. Tarashi's sword fell in the ring, but Min Cheng still had his Nun-Chucks in his hand. Tarashi was shocked because no one has ever done that before. Min Cheng said I told you I could handle a swordsman.

Tarashi said you got a weapon and I don't. Min Cheng said o.k. I'll make it fair. Min Cheng threw his Nun-Chucks down as he and Tarashi got into hand-to-hand combat.

They started fighting and Min Cheng still got the best of him. They both went into their animal rage. Min Cheng turned into his purple Dragon form. Tarashi turned into his tiger form. The crowd couldn't believe it. Tarashi charged and threw punches at Min Cheng but was blocked. Min Cheng punched and kicked Tarashi with combination blows. When Tarashi was too weak to punch and kick, Min Cheng opened his mouth and blew out a flame and set Tarashi on fire. After the flame disappeared, Tarashi fell on the ground as he turned back human.

Min Cheng walked up to him, turning back human at the same time. Tarashi was on his stomach. Min Cheng grabbed him by his right arm and twisted it. He asked, where is Redd Lion? Gray Wolf jumped in the ring and ran over to Tarashi. He said you heard him. Tell us where Redd Lion is. Tarashi said I'm not telling you.

Min Cheng twisted it a little harder until Tarashi hollered. He said tell us where Redd Lion is, and I will let you go.

Tarashi said O.K.! O.K.! He's in his mansion. Gray Wolf asked, where is the mansion? Tarashi said on Malvern Avenue, across the street from the Country Club. It's the biggest mansion in the neighborhood. Gray Wolf and Min Cheng looked and smiled at each other. Min Cheng let go of Tarashi's arm as he still laid in the ring. Gray Wolf and Min Cheng got out the ring as everybody cheered. The owner walked up to them.

He said you guys saved my Boys Club. I really appreciate you for doing that. He looked at Min Cheng and asked how did you guys turn into animals. Min Cheng said because we're all cursed with animal instincts.

Gray Wolf said not after tonight, we won't. The Kwawpaw fighters hugged and shook Min Cheng and Gray Wolf hands. Gray Wolf said now let's go and get Redd Lion, I know where he's at. Panthar said o.k. let's go.

As the Kwawpaw fighters were leaving, Gray Wolf and Min Cheng looked back at Tarashi and he was gone.

Min Cheng looked at Gray Wolf and said that's just like a Ninja. Gray Wolf said yep, playing possum.

The Kwawpaw fighters left the Boys Club to find Redd Lion.

Chapter 14

FINAL FINALE
GRAY WOLF VS. REDD LION

It's 9:30 at night. As they were riding on their way to Malvern Avenue, Gray Wolf started giving his fighters advice.

He said o.k. everybody, listen up. I know how Redd Lion think. He's going to send all of his fighters after me. He's going to want me to be so weak, that I can't lift a finger. Everybody that you fought; I need for you to challenge them again. I need enough energy to challenge Redd Lion. Tauro said o.k. Amigo, I'll fight Tommy. Brazen said I'll fight Cajun if he's there. Sheryl said of course, I got Catherine, I know she'll be there. Panthar said I got Guerilla; he needs to be off the streets. Min Cheng said Tarashi might be more dangerous than all of them. I'll challenge him again. He doesn't scare me. Gray Wolf said o.k. good, as long as we're organized, we'll have a better chance of winning and to get that medallion back. Brazen said we still got another day to get it. Gray Wolf said yeah, but we need to get it back as soon as possible. Brazen said o.k. I understand. Gray Wolf and the Kwawpaw fighters were on their way to Redd Lion's mansion.

At Redd Lion's mansion, there are bright lights and cameras on the outside of his mansion that Tarashi had set up. On the inside on the second floor are all of the Ahshitaw fighters. There's Tommy, Catherine, Guerilla, Cajun, and Tarashi. They all have their heads down because they're ashamed because they didn't take over any businesses. In front of them are twenty stairs. On the twentieth stair is a chair like that a king would sit in.

Redd Lion is sitting in the chair with a piece pipe in his hand, smoking. He's looking down at his fighters.

He said I can tell by the expression on all of your faces that you have failed me. He asked how many businesses any of you have taken. The Ahshitaw fighters looked at each other. Tommy looked up and said none.

Redd Lion got angry. He asked what you mean?! Tommy said Every time we tried to take over a business, that Indian guy and his fighters showed up and interrupted what we tried to do. Redd Lion asked what Indian guy and fighters? Tommy said he says his name is Gray Wolf. He has fighters that showed up at every business we tried to take over. Redd Lion stopped smoking his piece pipe and looked up. He said Gray Wolf! What does he look like?

Catherine said he has a white feather in the back of his head. He has black war paint across his eyes. He has hair that comes down to his shoulders. He's dressed in gray clothing. He says you have something that belongs to him.

Redd Lion grabbed the medallion around his neck. He said oh really! Yes, I do know him. I grew up with him. He's not weak. He's tougher than he looks. Catherine said I really think you made him very upset, especially if you have something that he wants. Redd Lion asked you said he has fighters with him. Guerilla said yeah, he even recruited one of my enemies. Tarashi asked, how did he know about every business we were supposed to have taken over?

Cajun reached in his pocket and noticed his map with all the names on it was gone, but he didn't say anything.

Redd lion said I don't know. Did any of you have the names of businesses that we were supposed to have taken?

Cajun lied. He said No, we didn't. Redd Lion said well he found out somehow. We got to stop him.

The intruder alarm went off. Redd Lion got his remote control and click the button on his T.V. screen. He saw Gray Wolf, Tauro, Brazen, Sheryl, Panthar, and Min Cheng. He said well speak of the devil. Gray Wolf and his fighters are in my front yard right now. Tommy said he's a bounty hunter. Redd Lion said yeah when he wants something bad enough, he won't stop until he gets it. Tarashi asked should we go and get them. Redd Lion said yeah, do what you must do, but bring Gray Wolf to me. Tarashi said o.k. we're on it.

All the Ahshitaw fighters ran out the door, downstairs to meet Gray Wolf and the Kwawpaw fighters.

Redd Lion sat back down in his chair. When he picked his piece pipe up to smoke, a flame of fire exploded behind him. When he turned around to see what it was, he noticed it was the spirit of his father, Chief Serpent. Redd Lion dropped his piece pipe and stood up. Chief Serpent still has the knife wound in his chest. He has handcuffs around his wrist that's chained down with shackles around his feet. Redd Lion asked, father is that really you? Chief Serpent said yes, it's really me. He said I need you to kill Gray Wolf so I can walk the earth forever. Redd Lion asked, are you in hell?

Chief Serpent said yes, and Nukpana still have some of us in chains. Redd Lion asked who is Nukpana.

Chief Serpent said he's a demon. He's worse than Lucifer. If you have a duel with Gray Wolf and lose, don't make any deals with Nukpana. If you win, he'll give you power. If you lose, he'll take your soul. This is what our ancestors went through. Redd Lion said o.k. I hear you.

Chief Serpent and the fire around him had disappeared. Redd Lion sat back down to smoke his piece pipe. Outside in front of the mansion, the Kwawpaw fighters are walking closer to the door. Brazen asked, so do we go and knock or what? As he was talking, the door opened and the Ahshitaw fighters came out. Gray Wolf said no, we don't have to, here they come. Tarashi stepped forward. He said tonight, all of you will meet your demise.

Min Cheng said I don't think so. Tarashi said I do. Gray Wolf asked, where is Redd Lion? Tarashi said he's inside, but you won't live to see him. Gray Wolf said well we'll see. The Kwawpaw fighters stood in front of Gray Wolf.

Tarashi yelled, Attack! The Ahshitaw fighters charged the Kwawpaw fighters. The Kwawpaw and Ahshitaw fighters were fighting. Gray Wolf ran around them and into the mansion.

When he went inside, he wasn't sure where Redd Lion was because all of the doors. He put his index finger to his temper to cut on his night vision to see if he could see where the most footprints came from. When he did, he saw all of the footprints coming from the left side of the stairs. Gray Wolf went up the stairs. He kept his finger on his temper until he got to the door where all of the Ahshitaw fighters came from. He took his finger off his temper. He started talking to himself. He said Redd Lion have to be in this room. He backed up a little and ignited electricity from both of his arms until it formed into lightning. Gray Wolf threw lightning from his arms and hit the doors. They exploded, "KABOOM!" Redd Lion dropped the piece pipe he was smoking.

Redd Lion asked, what is that? He stood up. Gray Wolf came walking through the door and walked in front of the stairs. He pointed his finger at Redd Lion and said, give me that medallion off your neck, it's not yours.

Redd Lion started laughing. He replied, you really think it's that easy. Like I'm a really just give It to you like that.

Gray Wolf said either give it to me or I'm taking it. Redd Lion started walking down the stairs. He said my ancestor's soul was in this medallion. Gray Wolf said o.k. well he's freed now, so give it here so I can restore the curse on earth. That's why you took it in the first place because you want earth to be cursed forever.

Redd Lion said you're right, I like the animal within me. I like the feeling of supreme power. I'm taking America back. This Is our land. Everybody still thinks Christopher Columbus discovered it when you know he didn't. Gray Wolf said yeah but you're going to make the federal government raid our tribes again, and I can't have that. Your father sent my father an invitation to battle and he lost fair- and- square. Redd Lion said my father didn't send your father an invitation. Your father is the one who sent it. Gray Wolf said no he didn't.

Redd Lion said you know what, you're right, he probably didn't because after I read the letter, I recognized the handwriting. It's your Uncle Hawk's handwriting. Gray Wolf said Uncle Hawk didn't send you an invitation!

Redd Lion pulled the letter out of his pocket and gave it to Gray Wolf. Redd Lion said look at the handwriting. Your Uncle Hawk set up the meeting on the mountaintop. Gray Wolf grabbed the letter to read. It said to Chief Serpent, please meet me between the Kwawpaw and Ahshitaw territory on the main mountaintop. I want to challenge you one more time to see who is stronger. The

Kwawpaw tribe has always been stronger than the Ahshitaw tribe.
Come on Monday morning between 12:00 or 12:30 P.M. I don't
care if you have a witness with you or not, Chief White Eagle.
Gray Wolf threw the letter down. He said that is the same kind
of letter we got, my father didn't write that letter. Redd Lion said
I know he didn't. Your Uncle Hawk did. He wanted your father
killed, so he can be the next Chief of the Kwawpaw tribe. The
reason why he sent you on this mission by yourself, because he
wants you to be killed because you are the only one standing in his
way. He didn't think you were going to recruit your fighters. He
doesn't care about this medallion. He wants this animal instinct
forever to.

Gray Wolf said I'll deal with my Uncle Hawk later, but now
I need that medallion and you're going to stop trying to take
over businesses. You sent one of your fighters to try and take our
land. Redd Lion said the only fighter I sent towards your area was
Tommy. He's stupid sometimes. I didn't send him to take over
your land by himself. I told him to challenge a fighter named
Tauro for his land. Gray Wolf said Tauro Is my friend. He's outside
now. He lives down the hill from me. That's Kwawpaw territory.
Now back to the necklace and medallion. Hand it over.

Redd Lion said you're not getting it. Gray Wolf said so be it,

I'll just have to challenge you for it.

Redd Lion said o.k. but if I win, I'm going to kill you. Gray

Wolf said o.k. well I rather die because I'm not leaving without it.

Redd Lion said I'm ready. Gray Wolf said I am too.

Gray Wolf and Redd Lion got into there fighting stances.

Gray Wolf rushed in swinging. Redd Lion blocked and dodged

his punches. He hit Gray Wolf with two hard punches to the left

and right side of his face.

Redd Lion said you better change your mind before this fight

is over with. Gray Wolf said, never!

He rushed in again. Redd Lion kicked his knee and hit him

with a punch to the right side of his face.

Gray Wolf yelled with pain. Redd Lion laughed. Gray Wolf got

angry and ignited electricity from both arms until they turn into

lightning. Redd Lion got wide eyed. Gray Wolf threw lightning

at Redd Lions feet, "KABOOM!"

Redd Lion was knocked to the ground. Gray Wolf rushed in,

jumped in the air and hit him in the face twice. When Redd Lion

stood back up, Gray Wolf kicked him in the chest as hard as he

could. Redd Lion went flying out of the right-side window. He was shocked by Gray Wolf's attack. He stood up as Gray Wolf came running for him.

Redd Lion through fireballs from his left and right arms. Gray Wolf dodged one fireball but was hit with the second one. The second fireball knocked him down and drained a lot of energy from him. Gray Wolf slowly got back on one knee. Redd Lion took it as a defeat. He said to Gray Wolf, you lost the first round. If you lose again, you're going to die.

Gray Wolf thought about the death of his father. When Redd Lion snatched off his medallion, Aiyana and how his Uncle Hawk betrayed the family. Gray Wolf energy was restored. He stood up and pulled off his jacket.

He said I'm not losing, and you won't kill me. Redd Lion said we'll see. They faced each other again.

Redd Lion rushed in swinging. Gray Wolf blocked his punches and swung back and hit him in the face. They punched and kicked each other, but this time Gray Wolf got the most licks in. They fought each other for ten seconds. Redd Lion threw his hands to the side and hollered. He let out a roar and turned into his lion animal form. He had bright red hair, red eyes, long sharp teeth, orange-yellowish skin, long black claws and paws.

He had a long tail. The hair at the end of his tail was red. He was so muscular, it seemed impossible for Gray Wolf to win. Gray Wolf turned into his Alaskan Wolf animal form. He looked at Redd Lion and started growling and showing his teeth. Redd Lion let out a deadly roar like he wanted to kill. He started talking to Gray Wolf.

He said I tried to warn you, now you're going to die. Gray Wolf said I'm not scared of death. Redd Lion said well, rest in peace.

Gray Wolf thought since he turned into his animal form first, if he can hold him off for ten seconds, and when he turns back human, he'll attack and defeat him.

Redd Lion charged in aggressively, punching and kicking. Gray Wolf blocked all his punches and kicks. Redd Lion did this for ten seconds. He turned back human, and when he did, Gray Wolf attacked him very aggressively.

He threw combination punches and kicks. He hit Redd Lion in the stomach and knocked the wind out of him.

When Redd Lion fell on one knee, Gray Wolf swung with a strong uppercut and knocked him off his feet.

Redd Lion was on his back. Gray Wolf walked up to him, turning back human at the same time.

Gray Wolf pointed his finger at him. He said I told you, you won't kill me.

Gray Wolf snatched off his father's medallion from around his neck.

He and Redd Lion animal spirits left their bodies and into the medallion. The Kwawpaw fighters had defeated the Ahshitaw fighters. All their animal spirits left their bodies and into the mansion to the medallion. They knew Gray Wolf had defeated Redd Lion. Every human being on planet earth animal spirits had left their bodies. The animal instincts curse had been reversed.

Back at the Kwawpaw territory. Hawk and Aiyana were outside by their tipi's. When their animal spirits left their bodies, Hawk got angry. He talked out loud and Aiyana heard him. He said oh no! Everything is ruined. Aiyana looked at him weirdly. Aiyana asked, what do you mean? Did you see what left our bodies? Why did that happen?

Hawk hesitated for a second. He said I don't know. Hawk knew; he just didn't want to say.

Back at Redd Lion's mansion.

Gray Wolf put the medallion around his neck. It's bright red again. He said to Redd Lion, now you and your fighters can disperse. It's over. Redd Lion said no we won't disperse. I'm going to get you for this.

Gray Wolf said yeah! Whatever! Gray Wolf turned his back to walk away. Redd Lion jumped up and swung at him. Gray Wolf ducked. He hit Redd Lion in the stomach, and in the face. Redd Lion fell off the mansion as he was hollering, no! Gray Wolf said you tried to sneak me. You never give up.

He picked his jacket up and went back in the mansion. He went downstairs to the first floor. Before he could make it to the door, Panthar came in smiling. He said you beat him, did you? Gray Wolf said yeah, I did as he showed Panthar the medallion as the bright red was glowing inside. Panthar asked, where is he?

Gray Wolf said he tried to sneak and punch me. I hit him and he fell off the mansion. Panthar said that's good as he reached in his jacket and pulled out the dynamite. He said I guess we don't need this anymore.

Gray Wolf said yeah, we can use it. We can destroy this mansion. Do you have a light? Panthar said yeah, I do.

Panthar gave Gray Wolf the dynamite and lighter. He lit the dynamite and threw it in the mansion. When he did, him and Panthar ran out the mansion. When they got outside, they told everybody to move. All the Ahshitaw fighters was laid out in the yard. The Kwawpaw fighters got out the way. The mansion exploded.

"KABOOM! KABOOM! KABOOM!", as the mansion collapsed.

The Kwawpaw fighters gathered up, getting ready to leave. The Ahshitaw fighters heard the explosives and was getting off the ground. Sheryl ran to Gray Wolf and gave him a hug. She said you did it. You're awesome!

Tauro said way to go Amigo. Brazen said you beat him like he owed you money. Min Cheng said you don't have to worry about Redd Lion and the Ahshitaw fighters anymore. There all defeated. Gray Wolf said you're right. Are you guys ready to go? All the Kwawpaw fighters said yes. They all went to Min Cheng's Suburban, got in and left.

Min Cheng said I'll drop all of you off anywhere you want to go. Anybody need to go anywhere in specific?

Sheryl said you can drop me off at the Arlington Hotel. Panthar said me too. Brazen said I'm going home.

Tauro said I live down the hill from Gray Wolf. Min Cheng said o.k. we're on the way.

Min Cheng drove to the Arlington Hotel. It only took ten minutes to get there. Sheryl was sitting in the front seat between Min Cheng and Gray Wolf. Panthar, Brazen, and Tauro was sitting in the back. When Min Cheng pulled up at the Arlington, Gray Wolf got out to let Sheryl out. She looked at Gray Wolf and gave him a big hug and a kiss on his jaw. She said thank you for saving my life. Anything you need, let me know. Gray Wolf said o.k. I sure will.

He sensed that Sheryl liked him. Panthar got out of the back seat and to the Arlington to. He said I'll see you guys later man.

The Kwawpaw fighters spoke back. Min Cheng drove to the icy mountains to drop Brazen off. When Min Cheng made it to Brazen's house. Tauro talked to him. He said I don't see how you live up here. It's too cold up here.

Brazen said I'm used to it. I've always liked cold weather. Tauro said I don't. Gray Wolf said see you later Brazen.

He replied o.k. you too. Brazen got out the Suburban and went inside. Min Cheng went to the Kwawpaw territory to drop Tauro off. It only took seven minutes to get there. Min Cheng pulled up at Tauro's house. He got out the Suburban and said, thanks guys.

I'll see you later. Min Cheng said o.k. Gray Wolf said thanks for
your help.

Tauro said any time Gray Wolf, as he went into his house. Min
Cheng drove up the hill to Gray Wolf's tipi. Before he made it,
there's the graveyard where his father, Chief White Eagle is buried.
Gray Wolf said to Min Cheng, I tell you what, can you drop me
off at this graveyard. Min Cheng asked, are you sure? It's almost
12 o' clock at night. Gray Wolf said yeah, I'm sure. Min Cheng
pulled in front of the graveyard. Gray Wolf got out, but he talked
to Min Cheng before he went to the graveyard. He said thanks for
all your help. Your fighting skills are sharp.

Min Cheng said you're welcome. Let me know if you hear
anything else about the Ahshitaw fighters.

Gray Wolf said o.k. I sure will. I don't think they'll be bothering
us soon. Min Cheng said I got that feeling to.

They shook hands. After that, Gray Wolf walked to Chief
White Eagle's grave. He talked to it.

He said hello father, I just got the medallion back. I told you I
would. May you rest in peace for now. Maybe one day I'll see you
again. Gray Wolf walked off and headed towards his tipi at his
Kwawpaw territory. When he did, he heard a voice behind him

call his name. Gray Wolf recognized the voice of his father. When he turned around, he saw his father's spirit standing in front of his grave. Gray Wolf walked up to him, saying hello.

Chief White Eagle asked, how are you? I'm fine. I'm not in no more pain. Gray Wolf said I'm sorry I distracted you when you were battling Chief Serpent. I'm the reason why he stabbed you. Chief White Eagle said no, it's not your fault. I knew how treacherous Chief Serpent was. I shouldn't have turned my back on him.

Gray Wolf said well one day, I'll see you again. I guess I'll let you rest now. Chief White Eagle said o.k. But do me a favor, tell your Uncle Hawk, I know what he did, and he's going to pay for his sins. Tell him to give you your second feather. You're closer to be the next Chief of the Kwawpaw tribe than he is. Gray Wolf said I have a good idea what you're talking about, but I will tell him. Chief White Eagle said o.k. Thank you. You know what, you're not just a warrior, but you're a man. You did exactly what needed to be done. Gray Wolf said thank you. I'll give Uncle Hawk your message.

Chief White Eagle shook his head like yes to Gray Wolf. He turned around and walked to his grave and disappeared. Gray

Wolf walked towards the Kwawpaw tipis. Aiyana was sitting down in front of her tipi with a flower in her hand. She looked out the corner of her eye and saw somebody walking toward her. She looked up and saw Gray Wolf. She jumped up and ran towards him. She hugged and kissed him. They were excited to see each other.

She looked down and saw the medallion around his neck. She said so, this is what you were talking about.

Gray Wolf said yes, it is. Aiyana asked why it's red on the inside. Gray Wolf said that's the animal instincts curse. If the medallion is removed from my neck, we'll be cursed again. Aiyana asked, so where is Redd Lion?

Gray Wolf said we battled on his mansion. He fell off of it after he tried to sneak attack me. Aiyana asked Is he dead. Gray Wolf said I don't know, but thanks to the brave fighters I recruited, we beat him and his fighters.

Aiyana said, really? Gray Wolf said yeah really. Where's Uncle Hawk? Have you seen him? Aiyana said he might be in his tipi. He's been acting strange. Gray Wolf said let's go find him.

Gray Wolf and Aiyana walked around the corner and saw his Uncle Hawk walking towards them. Hawk looked up and seen them. He walked up to Gray Wolf and Aiyana. Hawk asked, what have you done? Gray Wolf asked what do you mean what have I done? I recruited fighters and we tracked down Redd Lion and his fighters down and got the medallion back.

Hawk said you wasn't supposed to have put it on. You were supposed to have brought it to me. I'm supposed to be the next chief of the Kwawpaw tribe. Gray Wolf said well you should of came with me. Hawk said I couldn't, I had to stay here. Gray Wolf said no, you could of came, and I know you are the one responsible for setting the meeting up for my father and Chief Serpent to meet at the mountaintop. Redd Lion showed me the letter you wrote to Chief Serpent. I know your handwriting. You wanted me to come and try to get this medallion back because you thought I was going to get killed. If I die, then you become the next Chief of the Kwawpaw tribe. I can't believe you'll sacrifice your own family to get what you want. Aiyana looked at Hawk, as he said no, I didn't.

Gray Wolf said yes you did. On my way up here, I stopped at my father's grave. His spirit came and talked to me. He told me to tell you he knows what you did, and you're going to pay for your sins. He told me to tell you to give me my second feather. I'm closer to being the next Kwawpaw Chief. Hawk couldn't say anything at first. He angrily reached in his coat, pulled out a feather to give to Gray Wolf. Hawk said all I know is everything is ruined.

He walked away angry. Gray Wolf and Aiyana held hands and walked to their tipi. Gray Wolf said everything is back in order. Aiyana said yes, it is. Hawk is in his tipi. He looked at Gray Wolf and Aiyana. He talked to himself.

He said I'm going to get that medallion. I'm going to be the next Chief of the Kwawpaw tribe.

The End.

Coming Soon!

Indian Warfare 2: Redd Lion's Revenge!

To whom this may concern

Creator & Writer of J-Young Comics / J-Young Games

Indian Warfare can be adapted into film, cartoon, comic book, action figure toys, or video game. The reason I wrote this story is because all the characters that are out, there are none about Indians. Mine is the first one ever. Everything that you read and see are all my original ideas. Native American people have a passion for animals.

I thought about what would happen if they would turn into animals. I thought the best way they would turn into animals is if they're angered. So, something got to happen for them to turn into animals. So, I came up with the medallion curse so every human being in the world to change into animals. The sons of the Indian Chiefs are recruiting different nationality of fighters because different nationalities of fighters have different fighting styles.

I put a 110% of work off into this project. Please consider "Indian Warfare" to be the next project in American history. Send me an e-mail at blackmale0405@yahoo.com and tell me who is your favorite character and why.

All characters and screenplay are copyrighted by,

Library of Congress / 101 Independence Avenue SE / Washington, DC 20559 – 6000

Copyright number is / **VAuu001334744. Below are drawings of all the characters that are in the story.**

J-YOUNG GAMES PRESENTS:

INDIAN WARFARE

KWAWPAW TRIBE   *VS*   *AHSHITAW TRIBE*

INDIAN WARFARE
KWAWPAW TRIBE

CHIEF WHITE EAGLE (Gray Wolf's Father)

UNCLE HAWK
(Gray Wolf's Uncle)

AIYANA
(Gray Wolf's Girlfriend)

INDIAN WARFARE - KWAPAW FIGHTERS

GRAY WOLF

MIN CHENG

SHERYL

BRAZEN

PANTHAR

TAURO

INDIAN WARFARE - KWAPAW FIGHTERS
(Animal Form)

GRAY WOLF
(Alaskan Wolf)

MIN CHENG
(Dragon)

SHERYL
(Cheetah)

BRAZEN
(Polar Bear)

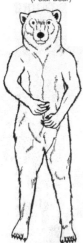

PANTHAR
(Black Panther)

TAURO
(Bull)

INDIAN WARFARE - NEUTRAL FIGHTERS

BLACK MALE

BLACK MALE (ROTTWEILER)

FARMER ED

FARMER ED (ROOSTER)

INDIAN WARFARE

CHIEF SERPENT
Ahshitaw Leader
(Redd Lion's Father)

INDIAN WARFARE - AHSHITAW FIGHTERS

REDD LION

TARASHI

CATHERINE

CAJUN

GUERILLA

TOMMY

INDIAN WARFARE - AHSHITAW FIGHTERS
(Animal Form)

REDD LION
(Lion)

TARASHI
(Tiger)

CATHERINE
(Cougar)

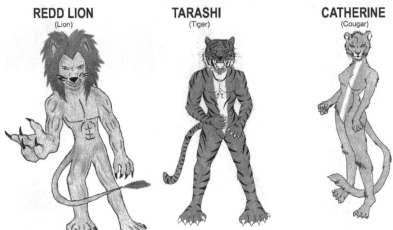

CAJUN
(Alligator)

GUERILLA
(Gorilla)

TOMMY
(Warthog)

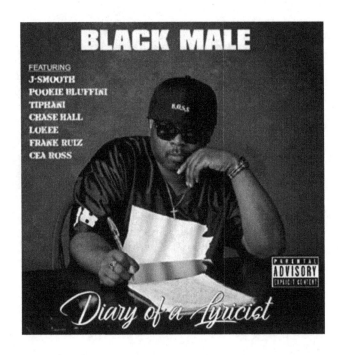

J-Young Shoe is available now on

www.aliveshoes.com/j-young-1

J-Young Clothing. Coming Soon!

Printed in the United States
by Baker & Taylor Publisher Services